The Witches of Bailiwick

By
Sandra Forrester

BARRON'S

All inquiries should be addressed to:
Barron's Educational Series, Inc.
250 Wireless Boulevard
Hauppauge, New York 11788
http://www.barronseduc.com

Library of Congress Catalog Card No.: 2004046349

International Standard Book No.: 0-7641-3025-0

Library of Congress Cataloging-in-Publication Data

Forrester, Sandra.
   The witches of Bailiwick / by Sandra Forrester.
      p. cm.—(Adventures of Beatrice Bailey)
   "Cover illustration and maps by Nancy Lane"—T.p. verso.
   Summary: To reverse the final part of the spell and free Bromwich from
Bailiwick Castle, Beatrice and her friends face many perils together, but she
must decide for herself whether to remain in the mortal world or move to
the Witches' Sphere.
   ISBN 0-7641-3025-0
   [1. Witches—Fiction.] I. Title.

PZ7.F7717Whe2005
[Fic]—dc22

                                                            2004046349

PRINTED IN THE UNITED STATES OF AMERICA
9 8 7 6 5 4 3 2 1

Contents

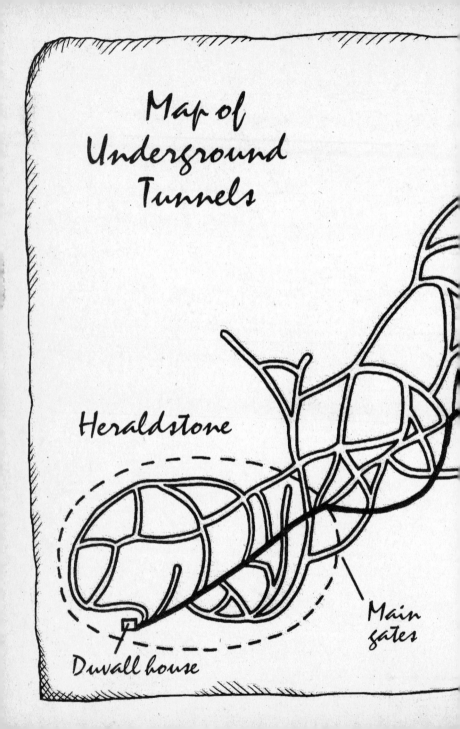

Map of Underground Tunnels

Heraldstone

Main gates

Duvall house

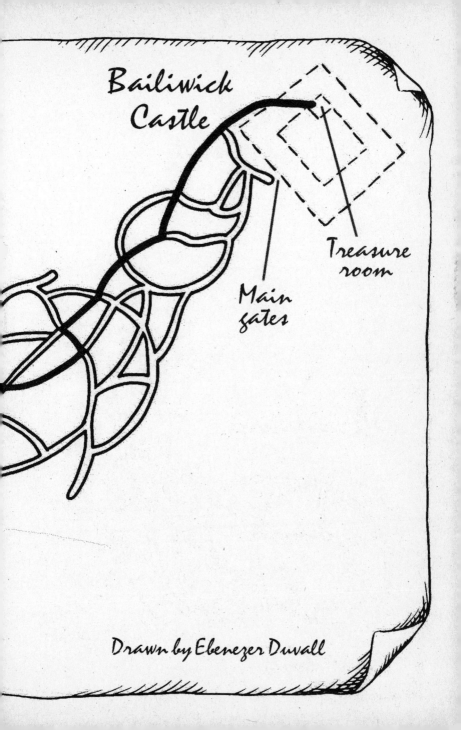

Bailiwick
Castle

Treasure
room

Main
gates

Drawn by Ebenezer Duvall

1

The Stranger

O n this dark, chilly afternoon in late October, Beatrice Bailey was admiring her neighbors' Halloween decorations as she walked to her best friend's house. Lawns were adorned with cornstalks and pots of flowers in autumn colors, and the glowing eyes of jack-o'-lanterns seemed to follow Beatrice down the street.

Beatrice didn't know it, but another pair of eyes was watching her, as well. Someone had been trailing her ever since she left her house—someone who was an expert at hiding behind trees and bushes, going unseen. And in any case, Beatrice was too preoccupied to notice the strange figure treading silently behind her.

School had closed for Fall Break that afternoon, and Beatrice and Teddy were celebrating by going to the mall. This had been Teddy's idea, of course, since she *lived* for clothes, whereas Beatrice was happiest in jeans and a T-shirt. Beatrice did like to browse in the bookstore, and she wanted to get some new toys for her cat, Cayenne, but she wasn't looking forward to spending this particular afternoon with Teddy—because her friend was beginning to get on her nerves! Ever since Beatrice's birthday party the previous weekend, Teddy had been obsessing over why the Witches' Executive Committee hadn't contacted them yet. "We always go back to the Witches' Sphere during mortal school breaks, so where are they this time?" Teddy had demanded at least a dozen times. "I was *sure* they'd show up on your birthday, like last year. Surely they aren't calling off the test at this late date. But why would they? We've shown them we can do it, Beatrice. What do you think's going on?"

Each time her friend had asked her this, Beatrice had just shaken her head. She had no idea what the Executive Committee was thinking, but she had to admit to herself that she would be secretly relieved if they *never* told her to return to the Sphere.

As a lot of people in town had come to suspect, Beatrice Bailey and Teddy Berry were witches. Beatrice might *look* like an ordinary thirteen-year-old—tall and skinny, with pale red hair cut straight across at the shoulder and silky bangs that habitually fell into her green-gold eyes—but as folks around town were fond of saying, looks can be deceiving. They didn't know it, but Beatrice's true name wasn't even Bailey; it was actually Bailiwick, but some long-ago ancestor had shortened the name to Bailey when he left his life as a Traditional witch in the Witches' Sphere and came to live here as a modern Reform witch. Being a witch in the mortal world was far from easy, as Beatrice, Teddy, and their two good friends, Ollie Tibbs and Cyrus Rascallion, could testify. As hard as they tried to fit in, some innocent attempt at magic always seemed to be blowing up in their faces, and there was usually a mortal audience to witness the fiasco. If they had been more *accomplished* witches (or not so inept, as Beatrice put it), they might have been able to hide their magical tendencies a little better, but each of the four friends could only cast one type of spell with any degree of proficiency. Which was why Beatrice had been so astonished when the Witches' Executive Committee had shown up on her twelfth birthday a year ago—*not* to give her the Everyday classification that she had expected, but to tell her they were going to test her magical abilities. If she passed the test, the committee would classify her as a Classical witch, which meant they considered her capable of working important magic.

Beatrice had been in a state of agitation and denial ever since. *Her*, a Classical witch? No way did she have that kind of talent! Nor did she especially *want* to be Classical. She would have been perfectly content as an Everyday witch like her parents. But then Teddy, Ollie, and Cyrus had offered to help her with the test, and the Executive Committee had agreed to reconsider their Everyday classifications if they succeeded. Beatrice's three friends had jumped at the chance to redeem themselves. And as if that hadn't put enough pressure on Beatrice, the committee devised a test that would give her the opportunity to help members of her family who had been imprisoned by the evil sorcerer Dally Rumpe for more than two hundred years. It was written in *The Bailiwick Family History* that the eldest female Bailiwick witch in each generation must try to break Dally Rumpe's spell. Beatrice happened to be the *only* female Bailiwick in her generation, so it had seemed the ideal test. And how could she possibly refuse to help her own flesh and blood? She had been forced by circumstances into agreeing to the committee's stupid test.

Even now, Beatrice wasn't sure how she and her friends had been able to break four parts of the spell—not to mention, come back alive! They had been in grave danger each time they traveled to the Sphere, but somehow, they had managed to pull it off. Now, with only one part of the test to go, Teddy just knew that they had those Classical classifications in their pockets. As Classical witches, Teddy was fond of reminding Beatrice, they would be able to go to a witch academy in the Sphere and learn all sorts of magic. Then they'd become Great Witches and be rich and famous and have ordinary Everyday witches lining up for their autographs.

As she approached Teddy's house, Beatrice shook her head, smiling in spite of herself. That Teddy! She was nothing if not an optimist.

Teddy's mother, who was an architect, had designed the Berrys' house. When their neighbors had seen this huge structure with massive steel beams and rounded concrete-and-glass walls begin to materialize amidst their traditional Victorians, they had gone into a panic. Now, fifteen years later, they still called it "that monstrosity."

Beatrice had started up the walk when she noticed movement out of the corner of her eye. But when she turned to look, all she saw was the nandina hedge that separated the Berrys' yard from their next-door neighbors'.

"Must have been a bird," Beatrice muttered, and continued toward the house. But she couldn't quite shake her feeling of uneasiness.

4

As Beatrice rang the doorbell, a hand slowly parted the branches of one of the nandinas, and a face appeared in the foliage. But the Berrys' front door had opened and Beatrice stepped inside, unaware of the sharp eyes boring into her back.

It was Teddy's mother who had come to the door. With her dark hair falling in a curly tangle past her shoulders, feet bare under a full red skirt that swished around her ankles, and at least twenty bangle bracelets on her slender arm, Beatrice thought she looked exotic and beautiful.

"Hi, Sweetie," Mrs. Berry said. "Teddy's in her room. Why don't you go on up?"

"Thanks, Mrs. B," Beatrice said, and headed for the spiral staircase that led to the second floor.

The first room at the top of the stairs belonged to Rupert, Teddy's eight-year-old brother. When she passed the open doorway, Beatrice saw Rupert's dark head bent over a row of glass beakers, from which was billowing an alarming amount of black smoke.

Beatrice stuck her head into the room. "Hi, Rupe. What are you doing?"

Rupert turned to look at her, his small serious face dominated by glasses with heavy black frames. "I'm using my Wily Wizard chemistry set to try out a spell I found in *Magic Weekly*," he said, pushing the glasses up on his nose.

"What kind of spell?" Beatrice was wary now, with good reason. Rupert had no more talent for magic than the rest of them, and any spell he cast could result in disaster.

"I'm making chocolate bars out of dirt and motor oil," he replied, and turned back to stir something in one of the beakers.

Beatrice peered at the beaker and saw that it contained a dark gooey substance resembling melted tar. "Well, good luck," she said hastily. And as she hurried down the hall to Teddy's room, Beatrice reminded herself to never eat chocolate in the Berry house.

Teddy was stretched out on her bed, surrounded by stacks of glossy booklets. She looked up from the one she was reading when Beatrice came through the door.

"What is all this stuff?" Beatrice asked.

Teddy held out the booklet in her hand and Beatrice saw what was printed on the front: *Dragon's Claw Witch Academy.*

Beatrice's eyes dropped to the other booklets on the bed. "Are all these—?"

"Yep," Teddy said with a grin. "Witch academy catalogs. I'm trying to decide where I want to go. I think I've narrowed it down to three: Dragon's Claw, Silver Willow, and Rowan Moon. Although Mystic Isle has beautiful beaches, and—"

"Wait a minute," Beatrice cut in. "This is totally premature, Teddy. You won't be accepted by a witch academy unless you're classified Classical, and you won't be reclassified until we finish the last part of the test—if then. And that's a big *if.*"

Teddy sighed and put down the catalog. She was petite and pretty, with short brown curls and dark eyes behind oversize wire-rimmed glasses. Right now those eyes were gazing at Beatrice with obvious annoyance.

"Beatrice, *must* you be so negative about this? The Executive Committee is going to send us back," Teddy said firmly. "I know they haven't contacted you yet, but they will. And we're going to ace this part of the test like we did all the other parts. And we're going to be classified Classical. Now, you can stay here and live a boring life among the mortals if you want to, but *I'm* going to the best witch academy I can find."

"I give up," Beatrice muttered.

The problem was, even if the committee did give her a Classical classification—which she still didn't believe would happen—Beatrice didn't know *what* she wanted to do. Why couldn't she be driven like Teddy? Or know for certain that life in the Witches' Sphere wasn't right for her? Why did everything have to be so complicated?

Teddy had stood up and was looking into the mirror as she brushed her hair. "By the way," she said casually, "have you heard from your cousin?"

"You mean Miranda? She e-mails me all the time."

Beatrice sat down on Teddy's bed and caught her friend's eyes in the mirror. Teddy's expression was perfectly neutral, a sure sign that she was bothered by something but trying to hide it.

"I know you didn't like Miranda at first," Beatrice said. "*None* of us did after all the stunts she pulled at Sea-Dragon Bay—but I thought you two had become buddies."

"Buddies? I wouldn't go that far," Teddy answered, brush poised in midair. "When she saved our lives and helped us break the spell on Blood Mountain, it did seem like she might have reformed. Still . . . she *was* working with Dally Rumpe when we first met her, wasn't she? Who's to say she won't go back to him?"

"After all she did to help us beat him? He was furious with her, Teddy. He wouldn't *take* her back. Besides, she's changed. She really is a good witch now."

Teddy raised her eyebrows. "Whatever you say. But I'll tell you this—Miranda Pengilly is the most ambitious witch I've ever known. If Dally Rumpe *did* approach her about switching back to his side, I just wonder what she'd do." Teddy turned around to face Beatrice. "And she's determined to go on this last trip with us, isn't she?"

Beatrice nodded. "She's almost as impatient to hear from the Executive Committee as someone *else* I could mention," Beatrice said dryly.

"Puh-*lease*," Teddy said, rolling her eyes. "Don't even think about comparing me to Miranda. Was *I* the one who made our hot-air balloon crash into the bay? Did *I* lock Ollie in a cellar so he'd drown when the tide came in? Did *I*—"

"No and no," Beatrice interrupted hastily, "and you didn't send those horrible rats after me or give yourself witch fever. Miranda did it all, but only because she didn't think it was fair that *I*, the younger cousin, was the one chosen to break Dally Rumpe's spell. And maybe it wasn't. Even though her name is Pengilly, she's more of a Bailiwick than I am. She's lived with them all her life, and I didn't even know they existed until a year ago. And, anyway, Miranda only *pretended* to support Dally Rumpe to get close enough to break his spell. I really believe that, Teddy. I trust her now."

Teddy sat down heavily beside Beatrice. "So do I," she said, but the admission came grudgingly. "I even like her—sort of. But she's the kind of witch who's going to steal the limelight if she can. When we break the final part of Dally Rumpe's spell, I'll bet Miranda finds a way to get most of the press coverage for herself. She's smart, you know, and beautiful, and—"

"But you're smart, too," Beatrice assured her. This rare sign of insecurity in her friend reminded Beatrice that no one, not even Teddy, was self-assured *all* the time. "And you're just as pretty as Miranda. Really, Teddy, if we're able to reverse the last part of the spell, there will be plenty of limelight to go around."

Then Beatrice blew her bangs out of her eyes and jumped up from the bed. "Are we going to stay here talking about Miranda all afternoon, or are we going to the mall?"

Teddy stood up and reached for her jacket. "You've discovered a foolproof way to make me forget my worries," she said, smiling a little. "Just point me in the direction of new clothes."

A light rain was falling when Beatrice and Teddy stepped outside.

"Can you take care of this before my hair frizzes?" Teddy asked.

"Sure," Beatrice said, and began to chant:

> *Circle of magic, hear my plea,*
> *Cloudy skies,*
> *Pesky rain,*
> *This I ask you: make them flee.*

Instantly, the rain ended and dark clouds began to retreat. But the sky was still gray as twilight approached, and streetlights were beginning to flicker on, one by one.

"Thanks," Teddy said. "I wish I could do something practical like casting weather spells."

"Your spell has saved us more than once," Beatrice replied as they started down the sidewalk in the direction of the mall. Little did she know that they would need Teddy's spell in just a few minutes.

Beatrice didn't realize at first that she was listening for footsteps; but unconsciously, she must have picked up on the faint sound of leather soles hitting the pavement. And she couldn't have said why, but when she did become aware that someone was walking behind them—someone who seemed to be gaining on them as the footsteps became more distinct— Beatrice's heart began to thump against her ribs. She couldn't remember a time in her life when walking anywhere in this town had frightened her, but she was frightened now.

"Teddy," Beatrice whispered, and her eyes darted sideways toward her friend.

Teddy seemed to be listening, too, her face tight and uneasy. "Are we being followed?" she whispered back.

"Only one way to find out," Beatrice said softly, and together, they spun around.

There was no one there. The sidewalk, the street, the surrounding yards deep in shadow all appeared to be empty.

"I know I heard someone," Teddy said.

"Do your spell and find out."

Teddy nodded and began to chant:

Candle, bell, and willow tree,
Who does stalk my friend and me?
Use your magic for our side,
Show us who would wish to hide.

Suddenly, a nearby clump of pampas grass sprang apart, revealing a man Beatrice had never seen before. He was crouched down, obviously trying to hide behind the tall shoots of grass, but Beatrice and Teddy could still see that his clothing was like nothing people wore in twenty-first century America—or in any other part of the mortal world. He was wearing a dark blue tunic made of some rough material over a full-sleeved shirt that had once been white but was now yellow with age. Brown trousers were stuffed into worn leather boots that came up to his knees, and a leather pouch was attached to his belt. His hair was dark and shaggy, falling over the collar of his shirt and into his eyes, but in the gathering twilight, it was difficult to see his face clearly.

"Who are you?" Beatrice demanded, her fear receding as anger took its place. "Why are you following us?"

As the man rose slowly to his feet, the streetlight illuminated his face. Beatrice and Teddy could see now that this stranger was not a full-grown man at all, wasn't, in fact, much older than the two of them. He was tall and very thin, with the gangly limbs and awkward stance of a boy. Then Beatrice noticed the beautiful dark eyes, nearly hidden by his rough hair, and she realized that he was handsome, or would be someday, when he grew into those strong features.

But there was no time to speculate about him, or to ask more questions, because the boy had started toward them. And he was holding a knife! Something dark and sinister flashed across his face, and he no longer appeared young.

Beatrice's fear returned, causing her legs to suddenly go weak and begin to tremble. She stared into those piercing eyes and wondered how she could have thought them beautiful.

"Run!" Teddy screamed.

But it was too late for that. The stranger had already reached out and grabbed Beatrice's arm, his strong fingers closing around her wrist. As she tried to pull away, he raised the knife into the air . . . and Beatrice knew.

He was going to stab her!

2

Thief!

Teddy screamed, "Don't kill her!" and abruptly, the boy's grip relaxed on Beatrice's wrist.

She jerked her arm free, prepared to run, but then she saw the expression on the stranger's face. He looked stunned.

"Kill her?" the boy repeated, sounding astonished. "Look here—I may be lots of things—some of them not polite to discuss in front of ladies—but I'm *no killer!*"

The color had risen in his face, and he was breathing hard as he glared at Teddy.

"Then what did you intend to do with that knife?" Beatrice burst out, her voice shaking.

The boy's eyes darted from Teddy's face to Beatrice's, and then to the weapon in his hand. He dropped his head, as though ashamed, and slowly returned the knife to its sheath on his belt.

"I don't go anywhere without my knife," he mumbled, "but I don't hurt anybody with it."

Teddy's eyes blazed. "You just make a practice of swinging it around, threatening people, but you don't use it. Forgive me if I find that hard to believe!"

The boy's face turned stony. "You don't have to believe it," he shot back. "Usually just showing people I *have* a knife makes them listen up."

Beatrice had partially recovered from her fright, and she found her curiosity taking over.

"Okay, we're listening," she said. "Who are you and where do you come from?"

He sighed, looking as if the past few minutes had been nearly as unsettling for him as they had been for the girls. "My name is Ganef," he said, looking steadily at Beatrice, "and I'm from the Witches' Sphere."

"Why doesn't *that* surprise me?" Beatrice muttered, and blew her bangs out of her eyes. "What part of the Sphere?"

"A town called Heraldstone. It's near the castle of Bailiwick."

Teddy became instantly alert. "Bromwich's castle," she said to Beatrice. "That's where we're supposed to go this time."

Beatrice nodded as she studied the boy's face. "So why are you here? Do you work for Dally Rumpe?"

Ganef was clearly shocked by the question. "*No!* He's evil—I'd never—*Look*," he said, spreading his hands wide as if asking for Beatrice to understand, "I'm no saint, all right? I'm a thief! Well, actually, a pickpocket—but I'm good at it," he added with noticeable pride, "and when I'm older, maybe I'll be good enough to be a full-fledged thief—but I don't harm people. And I'd *never* help Dally Rumpe with *his* dark deeds."

"All right," Beatrice said, "so why are you here?"

"I work for a man named Wolf," Ganef said. "He's the one who sent me to find you. And he told me to watch you for a while before introducing myself, to get a feel for how powerful your magic is."

Beatrice and Teddy exchanged a look.

"And did you?" Beatrice asked. "I mean, get a feel for how powerful we are?"

Ganef nodded solemnly. "I saw you make the rain stop, and I saw *her*," he said, jerking his head toward Teddy, "uncover my hiding place. From all appearances, you have strong powers. But Wolf suspected that all along—otherwise, how could you have won out over Dally Rumpe so many times? It has to be more than luck."

Beatrice felt laughter bubbling up inside her, but she managed to suppress it. So they had strong powers, did they? How quickly the pickpocket would change his mind if he knew that he had just witnessed the sum total of her and Teddy's magic.

"So Wolf sent you here," Teddy prompted impatiently.

"That's right," Ganef said. "See, Heraldstone's a rough place, left mostly to us outlaws. Thieves, pickpockets, highwaymen—we've got 'em all. Now the old-timers say, before Dally Rumpe cast his spell on the kingdom of Bailiwick and made Bromwich a prisoner in his own castle, that Heraldstone was a bustling place, 'a center of commerce,' they called it. But for the last two hundred years, since Dally Rumpe took over the castle and brought in all his ghouls, nobody wants to do business in Heraldstone. And most of the upstanding folks moved away long ago. So we're cut off from the rest of the Sphere—we don't even get newspapers, and not many visitors, either—and we wouldn't know anything that's going on beyond the town and the castle if it weren't for the highwaymen. They travel the roads far from Heraldstone looking for people to rob, and they come back and tell us what's happening. That's how Wolf knew about four witches breaking parts of Dally Rumpe's spell, and when he found out that you'd be coming to Bromwich's castle next, he decided to help you."

Ganef paused for breath and Beatrice regarded him warily. "Help us how?" she asked.

"By looking out for you," he said. "There's no place for you to stay except Heraldstone—it's the only town anywhere near the castle—but it's not safe for outsiders. Heraldstone has other gangs of thieves besides Wolf's who'd like nothing better than to hit you in the head for your shoes or a little change. But they respect Wolf," Ganef added, "and they fear him, too. If they know you're under his protection, they'll think twice before doing you any harm. Wolf says your only chance is to come and stay at his house."

Beatrice didn't like anything she was hearing. If Heraldstone was as bad as the young pickpocket said, she'd prefer to have no part of it. But if it was also true that there was no other place for Beatrice and her friends to stay, what choice did they have? But living with *thieves*? And this Wolf guy must be pretty tough if other thieves were afraid of him! *Wolf*. Even the name was disturbing.

"I guess this is a lot for you to take in," Ganef said. He spoke almost gently now, and his dark eyes seemed kind. "But Wolf is a man of his word. If he says he'll protect you, he will."

"You trust him then," Beatrice said.

Ganef shrugged. "Sure, and why not? My folks died a long time ago, and Wolf took me in. He's fed me and clothed me and taught me how to pick a pocket so quick, I'm on the other side of town before *my customer* knows he's been had." Ganef was grinning now, and he seemed far too young and good-natured to rob anyone.

"It was Wolf who named me Ganef," the boy went on, sounding quite cheerful now. "It means *thief*."

"What was your name before?" Teddy asked.

Ganef made a face. "*George*. Can you beat that? Sounds like a potbellied old banker or something. Ganef's much better!"

Beatrice wasn't so sure about *that*, but she kept her opinion to herself.

"So why does Wolf want to help us?" she asked bluntly. "Why should it matter to him if Dally Rumpe's spell is broken or not?"

"Because business is bad," Ganef said, shaking his head. "Let me tell you, it's hard to make a living picking pockets when most of the pockets are empty! Wolf says if Dally Rumpe went away, Heraldstone would begin to thrive again, and us thieves could make a killing. Of course," he went on, "there's some who like us being isolated, especially the highwaymen. After they've done their robbing, they come back to Heraldstone where there's no real law to speak of. It's a perfect hideout. Even some of Wolf's men aren't happy with the idea of things changing. They don't want you to come."

Beatrice nodded absently. In the past year, she had met quite a few resentful witches who had just wanted her

17

to go back where she'd come from and leave them in peace.

"Is that all you have to tell us?" she asked the boy.

"No, there's one more thing. Wolf thought you should know that there's been a lot of activity around Bromwich's castle lately. Wolf's men keep an eye out for anything unusual going on, and they've been reporting back that Dally Rumpe's bringing in whole armies of guards. Goblins, you know," the pickpocket added. "He's always used goblins to guard the castle walls, but more are coming every day."

"Why?" Teddy asked.

"Wolf thinks Dally Rumpe's getting ready for your arrival," Ganef said, his look at Teddy suggesting that she should have been able to figure this out for herself, "to make sure he doesn't lose again. This *is* his final chance, isn't it? Wolf says Dally Rumpe will stop at nothing to hold on to the last piece of Bailiwick."

"We should have expected as much." Beatrice appeared calm on the outside, but inside, her heart was racing and her stomach was doing flips.

"So what's your answer?" Ganef asked briskly. "Should I tell Wolf that you'll be staying with him?"

Beatrice hesitated, then said, "The Witches' Executive Committee decides when—or if—we return to the Sphere, but we haven't heard from them yet. And I need to discuss where we'll be staying with the committee before we make any plans."

Beatrice glanced at Teddy, who nodded, and then looked back at Ganef. She could tell from his expression that he was surprised by her answer.

18

"The committee advises us," Beatrice went on firmly, "and my friends and I can't make any decisions until we talk to them. But please tell Wolf that we appreciate his generous offer. Is there some way we can get in touch with him later?"

"He figured you might need time to think about it. Not that you have much choice," Ganef added bluntly. "But when you've made up your mind, you're to go to a shop here in town run by Mathias Snow. He'll see that Wolf gets your message."

"Mathias Snow," Beatrice murmured. "He has that antique shop on the other side of town. You mean, *he's* a witch?" she asked Ganef.

The boy nodded.

"Do you know him?" Teddy asked Beatrice.

"No, but Mom bought a desk from him a couple of years ago," Beatrice said. "I remember her saying that he's a very peculiar man."

"I have to be getting back," Ganef said, "so listen carefully. When you see Mathias Snow, you're to say, 'Do you sell wolves here? I'm looking for a rare one.' You got that?"

"Do you sell wolves here? I'm looking for a rare one," Beatrice repeated, smiling because it was so—theatrical! This Wolf seemed to be carrying the cloak-and-dagger stuff a little too far.

"That way, the old freebooter will know that you've really been in touch with Wolf," Ganef explained.

Beatrice raised her eyebrows. "Freebooter? What does that mean?"

"*Thief*," Ganef replied, grinning again, "or maybe more of a pirate. He did his share of robbing in

Heraldstone during Wolf's father's time. But in my opinion, once a thief, always a thief. What he charges for the junk in his shop is highway robbery!"

Beatrice and Teddy laughed, and Ganef looked pleased by their reaction. "Old Mathias will pass your decision along to Wolf," he said, "and if it's yes, I'll meet you at the antique shop and escort you to Heraldstone. Just give Mathias a date and time."

After their experience with a real-life, knife-carrying pickpocket, Beatrice and Teddy lost all interest in going to the mall. Teddy had been planning to spend the night with Beatrice—partly because she was sure that the Witches' Executive Committee would put in an appearance now that Fall Break had started—so the two girls went by Teddy's house to pick up the things she'd need, and then headed for Beatrice's house. This time, Beatrice was fairly certain that they weren't being followed.

The Baileys lived three blocks away, in a house that was big and old and white, with a wraparound porch. Except for the lime-green shutters and the glass witch balls hanging in the living-room window, Beatrice's house appeared quite ordinary compared to Teddy's.

The Baileys' dark green SUV was parked in the driveway, which meant that Mr. and Mrs. Bailey were home from work.

As they climbed the porch steps, Beatrice said, "Maybe they brought burgers," which was a polite way of saying that she hoped her mother wasn't cooking. Mrs. Bailey was a terrible cook, as was Mr. Bailey, for that matter.

"I'm glad Ollie and Cyrus are coming over for dinner," Teddy said, following Beatrice into the large front hall. "We'll be able to tell them about Ganef. They're never going to believe it."

"I'm not sure *I* believe it," Beatrice retorted.

About that time, a large, longhaired cat that was predominantly black, with dashes of orange and white, came padding down the hall to meet them.

"Hi, Cayenne," Beatrice said, and the cat leaped into her arms.

Closing green-gold eyes that looked remarkably like Beatrice's, Cayenne began to purr, a gravelly rumble that made her whole body vibrate.

Just then, they heard a burst of laughter from the kitchen.

"That's Ollie's laugh," Beatrice said. "I guess he and Cyrus came over early."

And sure enough, when Beatrice, Teddy, and Cayenne entered the kitchen, they found Ollie and Cyrus helping Beatrice's parents with dinner.

Mr. and Mrs. Bailey, who were standing at the counter chopping vegetables, wore identical khaki pants and forest-green shirts with *Bailey Nursery & Garden Center* embroidered across the front. They were both tall and skinny like Beatrice, but Mr. Bailey's thinning hair was brown, while Mrs. Bailey's was the same pale red as her daughter's. Cyrus, who was small and dark, with vivid blue eyes and an infectious smile, was stirring something in a pot on the stove.

Then Beatrice's eyes came to rest on Ollie, where they lingered. He was at the sink, filling a pot with water. Almost as skinny as Beatrice but half a head taller, Ollie had green eyes and a mop of butter-yellow hair. Beatrice thought he was the most handsome boy she had ever seen, not to mention the smartest and the most thoughtful. She had been aware of a subtle change in their relationship this past year, a shift from liking each other to *liking* each other, but they hadn't talked about it yet. All Beatrice knew was that she felt happier when Ollie was around. And judging by the delighted smile on his face when he saw her coming into the room, Ollie felt the same way.

"How does spaghetti sound?" Ollie asked, his eyes still on Beatrice.

"Terrific," Beatrice answered. Then she glanced at her mother. "But doesn't it take hours to make spaghetti sauce?"

"Not if you buy it in a jar already prepared," Mrs. Bailey said cheerfully. "All you have to do is heat it up. That's Cyrus's job. Your father and I are in charge of the salad."

"And I'm cooking the pasta," Ollie said.

He carried the pot of water to the stove and began to chant:

> *Heat of flame, heat of fire,*
> *Give to me my one desire.*
> *Boil this water, bubbling free,*
> *As my will, so mote it be!*

The pot of water began to boil.

Dinner was actually good! Beatrice was amazed. This might be the only time in her life when an edible meal had been prepared in this kitchen—even when spells were used—or maybe, *especially* when spells were used. Her parents' talent for magic was about equal to their cooking skills.

Beatrice and Teddy didn't mention their meeting with Ganef during the meal. By unspoken agreement, potentially threatening situations were never discussed in front of their parents. There was no need to make them worry more than they already did about their offsprings' trips to the Sphere. But after they had finished off the scrumptious pineapple cake Mrs. Bailey had bought at the bakery, and no one could eat another bite, Beatrice insisted that her parents go watch the evening news.

"We'll do the dishes," Beatrice said.

Her three friends chimed in their agreement, and Beatrice's parents declared that they were all priceless jewels before leaving for the living room.

Ollie peered down the hall after Mr. and Mrs. Bailey, and then closed the kitchen door.

"Okay," he said, turning to Beatrice, "what did you want to talk to us about?"

Beatrice blinked. "How did you know?"

Ollie grinned. "You seemed unusually anxious to get rid of your mom and dad. So out with it!"

While they washed and dried the dishes, Beatrice and Teddy told the boys about meeting Ganef and related everything he had said, ending with Wolf's offer to provide them with protection.

"Wow!" Cyrus said several times during the telling, his blue eyes huge. And when the girls had finished, he grinned and said, "This is going to be the most exciting trip yet. Just think, living in a den of thieves—what an adventure!"

Teddy gave him a sour look and said, "You *always* start out saying how exciting it's going to be, and then you end up just as scared as the rest of us."

"That's true," Cyrus agreed affably, "but it wouldn't be exciting if there was nothing to be scared of, would it?"

Teddy just rolled her eyes.

"I don't like the idea of depending on outlaws," Ollie said, frowning as he dried the last plate.

"I feel the same way," Beatrice said, "but I thought we could talk to Dr. Featherstone and Dr. Meadowmouse about it. Maybe they know something about Heraldstone and this Wolf character. Besides, they've always made arrangements for us to stay in a safe place."

"Yeah, they have," Teddy said, perking up.

"But all those goblins arriving at the castle doesn't sound good," Cyrus remarked. "Remember those two horrible border guards the first time we went to the Sphere? Weren't they goblins?"

"Trolls," Beatrice replied, "but I suspect that goblins aren't any prettier."

"Especially a whole castle full of them," Cyrus murmured.

But then Teddy said, "So what? We've gotten past werewolves and sea serpents and every other kind of loathsome creature anyone's ever heard of. We can manage some goblins."

"Ollie, you and Cyrus are going to stay for a while, aren't you?" Beatrice asked suddenly. "Until midnight? Just in case . . ."

"The Witches' Executive Committee comes," Ollie finished for her. "You bet. I brought some DVDs," he added, and pulled several from the pocket of his jacket.

"Great!" Teddy said, reaching for them, and then she squealed. "*Ollie!* Where did you get these? *Witch on the Run* and *The Warlock Who Wasn't There* just came out on DVD—and only in the Sphere! I read about them in *Today's Witch.*"

"My mom gets them mailed to her," Ollie said. "She lets me order anything I want."

They spent the rest of the evening watching movies, trying to keep Cayenne out of the popcorn, and listening to Teddy tell them everything she had read about the plots—and giving away the endings. Beatrice and Ollie took turns yelling, "*Teddy! We don't want to know!*"

But Beatrice was also surreptitiously glancing at her watch, wondering if the committee would be there tonight—or ever—and still half hoping that they wouldn't be. Finally, the grandfather clock in the hall began to sound the first of twenty-four strikes. Midnight.

Beatrice sat up abruptly and stopped the movie. Everyone glanced nervously at one another, not saying a word.

On the twenty-fourth strike, Beatrice saw the large ball of light floating in from the hall. The witches were here.

3

Beatrice Takes a Stand

T he ball of light exploded, creating a shower of falling stars and ribbons of light. After the smoke and dust had cleared, Beatrice could see that the full committee was there, thirteen witches wearing flowing robes and matching pointed hats in dazzling jewel-toned colors. Only one of the witches wore black, and that was Dr. Thaddeus Thigpin, Director of the Witches' Institute. He was stooped and gaunt, his craggy, unsmiling face framed by a shock of untidy white hair. His ice-blue eyes stabbed into Beatrice's face as she came to stand before the committee.

Teddy, Ollie, and Cyrus followed close on her heels, and Mr. and Mrs. Bailey, who had obviously heard the explosion, appeared in the doorway. Beatrice's parents looked apprehensive, as they always did when they were about to hear that their only child was setting off for one of the darkest and most dangerous regions in the Witches' Sphere. It didn't help that one of the committee members, Dr. Aura Featherstone, was an old friend of Mrs. Bailey's. Perhaps it should have, but as far as Mrs. Bailey was concerned, Aura Featherstone was irritatingly cavalier about Beatrice coming face-to-face with the most evil sorcerer in the Sphere.

Beatrice's eyes eased away from Dr. Thigpin's penetrating stare and sought a more friendly face. Behind the Institute director was Dr. Featherstone, who could be quite imposing but had always been Beatrice's staunchest ally on the committee. The thirty-something witch was tall and uncommonly attractive, with auburn hair spilling over the shoulders of her jade-green robes. Beatrice thought she detected something unfamiliar in the witch's expression— Was it worry casting its shadow over her face?—but nonetheless, Dr. Featherstone had an encouraging smile for Beatrice. And there was Dr. Meadowmouse, another loyal friend. Dressed in saffron-yellow robes, Leopold Meadowmouse had a long, homely face and brown hair that stood out from his head like a toadstool. He, too, was smiling at Beatrice, radiating kindness and goodwill. The rest of the committee just looked bored.

"So," Dr. Thigpin said curtly, the word coming out like a bark, "here we are again, Beatrice Bailiwick."

Then he stopped, and Beatrice waited on pins and needles for him to continue. She could feel the tension building around her, as her parents and friends also waited anxiously for Dr. Thigpin to announce that it was time to return to the Witches' Sphere. But when he finally spoke, no one was prepared for what he had to say.

"We have a problem," the Institute director said bluntly. "You were supposed to go to Bailiwick Castle for the final part of your test, but that won't be possible now."

For a split second, Beatrice didn't react—surely, she hadn't heard him correctly—but then she saw her friends' shocked faces and realized that she hadn't misunderstood.

"We aren't going to Bromwich's castle?" Beatrice asked. She glanced at Dr. Featherstone, who now looked blatantly unhappy, and then at Dr. Meadowmouse, who appeared very solemn, indeed. "Are you canceling the test?"

"Not canceling," Dr. Thigpin said. "We're *delaying* it. Perhaps indefinitely, which would amount to the same thing as a cancellation, I suppose. It's too dangerous," he said, his bushy white eyebrows pinched together as he gave Beatrice an especially stern look.

"But our trips to the Sphere have always been dangerous," Teddy protested.

Dr. Thigpin glared briefly at Teddy, ensuring her silence, and then said to Beatrice, "Our intelligence sources have reported disturbing activities at Bailiwick Castle. Dally Rumpe has brought in a mass of armed goblins to guard the castle. It's obvious that he doesn't intend for you to win again. And while I understand that you've always faced danger in the Sphere, you wouldn't stand a chance this time. Your astounding good luck—or *whatever* it is that has allowed you to best Dally Rumpe—simply wouldn't be enough against all those goblins. You wouldn't even make it to the castle walls."

So they're finally letting me off the hook, Beatrice thought. *I don't have to go back to the Sphere. But that* didn't change one important fact, a detail that she sometimes tried to forget but couldn't for very long: She had given her word to Bromwich's daughters that she would do everything she could to break the last part of the spell and free their father. The strain on Beatrice's face reflected the conflict she was feeling. Here she was being handed an honorable way out—by the Director of the Witches' Institute, no less—but she had made a commitment to Bromwich and his daughters. *And a promise,* Beatrice thought with a sigh, *is a promise.*

She looked at her friends again, at Ollie and Cyrus's disappointed faces and Teddy's belligerent one. And she saw that Teddy was fighting hard to control herself, but was about to lose the battle.

"You *never* believed we could break the spell," Teddy said suddenly to Dr. Thigpin. She spoke quietly, but her voice shook with emotion. "*Everyone* thought we'd fail. But we didn't. And whether we succeeded because of luck or because we just wouldn't give up, we still succeeded. And I think calling off the test now is totally unfair!"

Teddy stopped at this point—probably, Beatrice suspected, before she burst into tears. Teddy's eyes *did* look suspiciously bright.

Dr. Thigpin's face had turned red, the lines of his natural scowl had deepened, and—for once—he seemed at a loss for words.

So into the silence, Beatrice found herself saying, "You all know that I've had mixed feelings about the test, and it may be true that we can expect greater danger this time, but we can't just forget that Bromwich is still a prisoner. His daughters need him, and we—" Beatrice glanced at her friends, "we need to try to finish what we started. I can't speak for everyone else, but that's what *I* think."

"So do I," Ollie said stoutly, and came to stand beside her.

Teddy was clearly startled by Beatrice's words, but then her face lit up and she hurried to Beatrice's other side. "I agree," she said.

"Me, too," Cyrus declared, and took his place beside Teddy.

Beatrice saw Dr. Featherstone's face relax, and then the witch beamed her approval at Beatrice. Dr. Meadowmouse was regarding her with admiration, and even Dr. Thigpin's expression seemed to have softened, though just barely.

"Oh, Beatrice," Mrs. Bailey said, the words coming out like a low moan. "Haven't you done enough?"

Beatrice looked at her mother and father, whose faces were tight with fear for her, and felt miserable. "I'm sorry," she said. "I don't want you to worry—but I have to do this."

Mrs. Bailey stared hard at Beatrice for a moment, and then her body sagged and her panicked expression dissolved into one of unhappy resignation. Mr. Bailey's nod was jerky, but he made an effort to smile at his daughter. Beatrice saw that as much as they dreaded her going, they understood why she had to.

Turning back to Dr. Thigpin, she said, "I know you have the authority to call off the test, but you can't bar us from the Sphere, can you?"

Dr. Thigpin made a sound like a growl in his throat, and Beatrice was sure she was in for the tongue-lashing of her life. But when the Institute director finally spoke, he sounded surprisingly calm.

"As a matter of fact," Dr. Thigpin said, "I *can* bar you from the Sphere, if I so choose."

Dr. Featherstone moved quickly to his side. "Thaddeus," she said anxiously.

"Oh, for pity's sake, Aura," Dr. Thigpin grumbled, "I'm not going to prevent them from returning to the Sphere. *But,*" he added, impaling Beatrice with his eyes, "as Director of the Witches' Institute, it is my duty to cancel the last part of your test and to advise you to stay away from Bromwich's castle for your own good. As a private citizen, however, I must admit that I find your perseverance and sense of responsibility admirable, Beatrice Bailiwick."

His scowl was more pronounced than ever, but the ice in his eyes had melted to a point where they seemed almost warm. *Almost.*

Beatrice was astounded. And pleased. A compliment from the curmudgeonly Dr. Thigpin was something to be treasured.

Ollie and Cyrus were smiling, but Teddy looked devastated.

"You mean," Teddy said slowly, "that we'll be risking our lives with no hope of being reclassified?"

"You don't *have* to risk anything," Dr. Thigpin responded curtly. "I've advised you to stay home. It's up to you."

Beatrice could almost see the wheels turning in Teddy's head. She could imagine her friend thinking that, if they were successful, the committee might still give them Classical classifications, test or no test. But there was no guarantee of that, so were the risks worth taking? Beatrice thought she knew what conclusion her daring and determined friend would reach, and she wasn't disappointed.

Teddy turned to Beatrice, chin raised defiantly, and said, "Who cares about the test? I want to go."

Just then, a witch who was no more than four feet tall and dressed in brown robes a size too large, elbowed his way through the assembled committee until he was standing beside Dr. Featherstone. It was Peregrine, Beatrice's witch adviser. His diminutive stature and those large ears protruding through his toast-colored hair made him look more like an elf than a witch; but Beatrice had learned that, despite his size and shy demeanor, he was fiercely devoted to his friends.

Beatrice smiled at Peregrine and received a lopsided smile in return.

Dr. Featherstone looked down when she felt a tug on her sleeve. "Yes, Peregrine," she said impatiently, "what is it?"

"I just wanted to say," the small witch mumbled, looking down at his long skinny feet, "that whether they're being tested or not, I'd like to escort Beatrice and her friends to the Sphere, as I always have."

"Certainly not!" came Dr. Thigpin's emphatic reply. "You are employed by the Institute, and we cannot officially support this endeavor. If they insist upon going, they go on their own."

Peregrine lifted his eyes and looked steadily into the director's face. "Beatrice Bailey and her friends stood by me when I was unjustly accused of working for Dally Rumpe," he said. "I can't turn my back on them now."

Dr. Thigpin's color began to rise again. "Then you have a choice to make," he said coldly. "It's either them or your job. Let me know what you decide."

Peregrine reached inside his robes and produced a plastic card with a clip on the end.

"Your Institute ID?" Dr. Featherstone looked stunned. "Peregrine, you need to think about this."

"There's nothing to think about," Peregrine said. He handed the ID to Dr. Thigpin, who grabbed it angrily. "Please accept my resignation, sir."

"No, Peregrine!" Beatrice exclaimed. "You can't give up your job. Not on our account."

Peregrine just shrugged and folded his arms across his narrow chest. Not only did the compulsively shy witch not look the least bit timid, he appeared downright combative at the moment.

"I won't let you do this," Beatrice insisted. "And, anyway, someone else has offered to escort us to the Sphere."

Now all faces were turned toward Beatrice, some clearly startled, and Peregrine's the most astonished of all.

"*Who* has offered to escort you?" Dr. Featherstone demanded.

"A thief named Ganef," Beatrice said, and then hearing the gasp from her mother, added quickly, "well, he's really just a pickpocket, and he followed Teddy and me when we were going to the mall, and—" Beatrice stopped when she saw the horror on her parents' faces. "Maybe I'd better start at the beginning," she said.

"Maybe you *had* better," Dr. Featherstone said, looking rather horrified herself.

Beatrice told them about meeting Ganef, what he had said about Heraldstone being unsafe for outsiders, and Wolf's offer to provide them with protection.

"Why didn't you tell us all this?" Mr. Bailey demanded. Mrs. Bailey seemed incapable of speech at this point.

Beatrice opened her mouth to say something, but Dr. Featherstone beat her to the punch. "Wolf Duvall," she said to Dr. Meadowmouse. "Remember him?"

"Arrested for robbery a few years ago," Dr. Meadowmouse replied, frowning as he tried to recall the details, "but the case was dismissed, wasn't it?"

"That case and about twenty before it," Dr. Featherstone retorted. "He's slippery, that one."

"Well, there's no way Beatrice is going to stay with thieves!" Mrs. Bailey burst out.

"Actually," Dr. Featherstone said slowly, "it might not be such a bad idea. It's true that Heraldstone is the only town anywhere near the castle, so they'd have to stay there. And all of the inns have been closed since Dally Rumpe took over. But from what I hear, Wolf Duvall lives very well. His house would probably be quite comfortable, and he's pretty much in charge in Heraldstone. If anyone can protect Beatrice and her friends, he can. And there's never been even a hint that Wolf is involved with Dally Rumpe."

"But he's a *criminal!*" Mrs. Bailey cried. "Really, Aura, you've gone too far this time."

Aura Featherstone frowned at her old friend, and then she said, "You're probably right, Nina. It *would* be best if Beatrice and the others didn't go to Heraldstone. However," she added, glancing at Beatrice, "it seems that your daughter has vetoed that idea. So what we have to think about is where they will be safest."

"If this pickpocket is going to escort you," Peregrine said to Beatrice, "then you don't need me."

"It isn't that we don't need you," Beatrice said quickly, noting the hurt look in Peregrine's eyes. "We never would have made it through the first part of the test without you. And you've become much more than my witch adviser. You're our friend."

Peregrine's eyes filled with tears, and he sniffed loudly. "But friends look out for one another," he said softly.

"You have," Beatrice assured him, "and you will again. But I can't let you lose your job. It means too much to you. And, Peregrine, I'll never forget that you were willing to give it up for us."

In the end, it was decided that Beatrice and her friends would accept Wolf's offer of protection and allow Ganef to escort them to the Sphere. Dr. Thigpin, by this time, was as ill-humored as Beatrice had ever seen him. He flung Peregrine's ID at him, and said sarcastically, "Your loyalty is heartwarming, I'm sure, but the next time you pull a stunt like this, you're fired!"

Beatrice caught Peregrine's eye and winked. The witch adviser blushed and ducked his head—but not before Beatrice saw his crooked smile.

"All right then," Dr. Featherstone said briskly, "let's tell these kids what they're going to be facing at Bailiwick

Castle." Then she turned to Dr. Thigpin. "Unless you have any objections, Thaddeus."

Dr. Thigpin scowled. "Technically, we shouldn't even be here. But since we are, I suppose there's nothing wrong with talking casually about Bailiwick Castle. You won't need me for that, will you?"

"No, Thaddeus," Dr. Featherstone replied. "Leopold, Peregrine, and I can handle it."

"Well, don't stay too long," Dr. Thigpin said crossly. "We don't want to be accused of encouraging them, do we?"

"No, Thaddeus, we certainly don't," Dr. Featherstone said agreeably.

"Very well. All those ready to return to the Sphere, think 'Home again, home again,'" Dr. Thigpin announced. And in the next instant, most of the committee members vanished into thin air. Only Dr. Featherstone, Dr. Meadowmouse, and Peregrine were left.

"Let's begin, Leopold," Dr. Featherstone said.

Dr. Meadowmouse looked across the room at an old black book on Mr. Bailey's desk. Suddenly, the book flew through the air into Dr. Meadowmouse's hands. Its faded leather binding creaked as the book fell open, and several large black beetles crawled out and began to climb up his arm.

"Beatrice, as you know," Dr. Meadowmouse said, "this is *The Bailiwick Family History*. You're familiar with most of its contents, but I'm required to remind you that you are charged with breaking Dally Rumpe's evil spell on the kingdom of Bailiwick. As a result of the spell, Dally Rumpe's brother, the good sorcerer Bromwich, and

Bromwich's four daughters have been held captive for more than two hundred years. You and your friends," Dr. Meadowmouse continued, "have reversed the spell on four regions of Bailiwick, and in so doing, have freed Bromwich's daughters. All that remains is for you to travel to the central region, where Bailiwick Castle stands, and repeat the counterspell in Bromwich's presence. If you succeed, the five regions of Bailiwick will be reunited, and Bromwich will be freed from the dungeon where he's imprisoned."

"I see no need to repeat what Beatrice already knows," Dr. Featherstone said crisply.

"Aura, surely you're aware that I'm required by witch law to do this," Dr. Meadowmouse replied.

"But *officially* we aren't even here," Dr. Featherstone reminded him, "so let's cut to the chase. Beatrice knows what she has to do. You just need to tell her about the obstacles she'll face."

Dr. Meadowmouse preferred to do things by the book, but he sighed and said, "Very well, Aura."

He flipped through some pages, searching for the right part. "Ah, here we are—Bailiwick Castle," Dr. Meadowmouse said, his eyes traveling down the page. "The castle is surrounded by a moat that is twenty feet wide. There's a bridge over the moat, but unfortunately, the bridge is enchanted. Anyone stepping on it will be shaken off into the water, which is inhabited by giant flesh-eating fish."

"What about the goblins?" Dr. Featherstone asked. "They won't even be able to reach the bridge with goblins on guard."

"That's probably true," Dr. Meadowmouse replied, turning to the next page. "The castle is surrounded by a stone wall that's thirty feet high. Atop the wall are goblins who watch the surrounding countryside and shoot flaming arrows at anyone who approaches the castle. If anyone *should* make it inside—although I don't see how that's possible," Dr. Meadowmouse murmured, "more armed goblins patrol the corridors, and creatures called Furies lurk in dark corners, waiting to fly out at intruders."

"Like bats?" Cyrus asked.

"Oh, no," Dr. Featherstone replied. "Furies are more like—ghosts, I suppose—only they're black, with horrible glowing eyes, and their touch can kill you."

"Oh," Cyrus said in a small voice.

"Well, what else is in the castle?" Teddy asked.

"Zortag," Dr. Meadowmouse answered as he studied a passage. "That's the name of an evil spirit that can take the form of a man but isn't really human. He stands guard outside Bromwich's cell, and it says here that he's so terrible, even the goblins steer clear of him."

"What does he look like?" Beatrice asked.

"He's seven feet tall, with gray skin and hair, and he wears gray, tattered robes," Dr. Meadowmouse replied. He turned another page. "Oh, yes, and he has one large red eye in the center of his forehead."

"Guess we can't miss him," Ollie said with a nervous laugh. "So what does *he* do to intruders?"

"If they look directly into his eye, they're paralyzed," Dr. Meadowmouse answered. "He's also strong enough to squeeze the life out of a witch with his bare hands—but he rarely resorts to that because he prefers to roast them live on a spit."

"Oh, he cooks, too," Cyrus murmured.

"And then, of course, there's the castle structure itself," Dr. Featherstone pointed out. "I've heard that the corridors form a sort of maze, and it's quite easy to get lost." She was beginning to look worried again. "Beatrice, keep that in mind and mark your path in some way so you won't keep going around in circles. And you'll have to go down below the castle to find the dungeon where Bromwich is imprisoned."

"Peregrine, do you have the map?" Dr. Meadowmouse asked.

Peregrine withdrew a sheet of rolled-up parchment from inside his robes and spread it out on the desk. Everyone moved closer to look at the map.

There it is, Beatrice thought, *Bailiwick Castle*. And just west of the castle was a cluster of buildings surrounded by a wall with the word *Heraldstone* printed above it.

"You said the pickpocket told you about the town?" Dr. Featherstone asked Beatrice.

Beatrice nodded.

"Well, I don't know very much, anyway," Dr. Featherstone admitted. "I've never talked to anyone who's been there."

"All I've heard is that Heraldstone is the domain of outlaws," Dr. Meadowmouse said.

Both he and Dr. Featherstone were looking at Beatrice and her friends with genuine concern.

"Always before," Dr. Featherstone said, "we've known that you were staying among friends. But this time . . ."

She placed a hand lightly on Beatrice's shoulder. "Maybe you *should* reconsider."

"Yes, Beatrice," Mrs. Bailey said quickly. "You see? Even Dr. Featherstone is afraid it's too dangerous."

Aura Featherstone frowned. "Don't put words in my mouth, Nina."

"Please," Beatrice said, "don't argue. It's our decision, and we've decided to go ahead with it."

"That's right," Teddy said, and Ollie and Cyrus nodded.

But all four of the adventurers, and even Cayenne perched on Beatrice's shoulder, appeared uncharacteristically subdued.

Beatrice was thinking that this trip was starting out like none of the others. The committee was advising them *not* to go, they wouldn't have Peregrine to bolster their morale, and they were going to be depending on *outlaws* for their safety. She couldn't help but wonder if they were doing the right thing.

Just then, Peregrine came over to Beatrice and handed her the map. "You might need this," he said. "And it's autumn where you'll be going, too, but colder than here. Don't forget to take heavy jackets."

The witch adviser was teary-eyed again, and Beatrice was afraid she might well up herself.

"When we break the spell," Beatrice whispered to Peregrine, "will you come to Bailiwick Castle and celebrate with us?"

Peregrine must have been aware that this was the first time Beatrice had ever said *When we break the spell*, not *If*. And he also must have realized that this sudden confidence was mostly bravado to make *him* feel better.

Peregrine swallowed hard, and then he said, "Nothing could keep me away."

The following morning, Beatrice sent an e-mail to Miranda, giving her a condensed version of everything that had happened, and telling her that they planned to leave for the Sphere on Monday morning at dawn. Almost immediately, she received her cousin's reply: *I'll be there*. M.

Beatrice, Teddy, Ollie, and Cyrus stood on the corner looking at the shop across the street. A large sign lettered in black and gold script read: *Mathias Snow Antiques*. But the sign's paint was faded and beginning to chip off. And the glass in the shop's front window was so streaked and dirty, it was hard to see the arrangement of merchandise on the other side. The place gave the appearance of neglect, but there was nothing frightening about it. *So why*, Beatrice wondered, *are we hesitating to go inside?*

"Let's get this over with," she said, and started across the street.

A bell jingled when Beatrice opened the door, and the odors of dust and dampness filled her nostrils as she entered the shop. Behind her, Teddy muttered, "Smells like there's been a flood in here."

Beatrice usually liked antique shops, but there was so much *stuff* piled up on every surface, and even hanging from hooks on the ceiling, she began to feel claustrophobic. Plus, it was awfully dark, the only light coming from a few small antique lamps scattered around the room and the little daylight that could penetrate through the dirt on the window.

There was practically no space to walk between the stacks of books and old trunks filled with everything from vintage clothing to porcelain dolls, but Beatrice managed to ease past two tables stacked high with china figurines without breaking anything. Then she hit her ankle on a cast-iron doorstop that resembled an enraged gargoyle. Pain shot up her leg and Beatrice grabbed her calf, trying not to whimper.

"Are you okay?" Ollie asked, taking hold of her elbow.

And that was when, with Beatrice hopping around on one foot and grimacing with pain, Mathias Snow chose to put in an appearance.

"May I help you?"

Beatrice jumped at the sound of the deep and unexpected voice, nearly falling into a Chinese folding screen as she jerked her head around. The man was standing only a few feet away, completely surrounded by assorted chairs, tables, and armoires. There was no way a mortal could have reached that corner without walking past Beatrice and her friends—which he hadn't, because they would have seen him—but, of course, Mathias Snow was a witch. *And a pretty creepy one, at that,* Beatrice thought.

He was wearing a wine-colored velvet jacket with stains down the front, and his silver-streaked blond hair looked as if it hadn't been washed in a very long time. There was even a bit of egg—or *something*—clinging to his droopy mustache. But aside from the hygiene issues, what bothered Beatrice most was the way he was looking at them. *Leering*, actually. And there was nothing warm about his smile. It was sly and secretive and made the hairs stand up on Beatrice's neck.

But . . . they had to be here if they intended to go to Heraldstone, and so Beatrice did her best to appear relaxed.

"Do you sell wolves here?" she asked the shop owner, and that struck her as sounding so funny, she had to glance away from his face to maintain her composure. "I'm looking for a rare one."

"I know of a *very* rare wolf," Mathias Snow answered, his voice turning silky, which made him seem even creepier to Beatrice. "Do you have a message for him?"

Beatrice handed the man a sheet of paper.

Mathias Snow read the brief message to himself and then looked up, his expression more devious and crafty than ever. "I'll see that our wolf gets this," he said, speaking barely above a whisper.

"Thank you," Beatrice replied, and started for the door. She couldn't wait to leave this place.

Once outside, Teddy asked, "Did you see the ring he was wearing? If that was a real emerald, it must be worth a fortune."

Beatrice just stared at Teddy. "Is that all you noticed?" she demanded. "His *jewelry?*"

"Well, you have to admit," Teddy said, "his *clothes* weren't much."

4

Robbers' Mile

It was still dark when Beatrice dragged her bulging backpack out to the porch to wait for Miranda and her friends. Cayenne dashed through the door behind her, followed by Mr. and Mrs. Bailey.

"Here they come," Beatrice said, catching sight of Teddy, Ollie, and Cyrus as they passed under a streetlight.

"Good morning!" Teddy called out, waving to the Baileys. There was an excited bounce in her step as she and the boys came up the front walk.

"Miranda isn't here yet?" Teddy asked, dumping her own backpack on the steps. Beatrice thought she sounded hopeful.

"She's coming," Beatrice said.

"Oh, okay," Teddy replied, sounding resigned.

"How long before we're supposed to meet Ganef?" Cyrus asked, his blue eyes sparkling in the porch light.

"Forty-five minutes," Ollie said. "We have plenty of time."

"It'll take us half an hour to walk to the antique shop," Teddy said, "so Miranda had better get here soon."

As if on cue, a tall, slender figure turned the corner and came striding down the street toward the Baileys' house.

Beatrice picked up Cayenne and placed her gently in the pocket of her backpack, so that only the cat's head was visible. Beatrice's mother began to hand out lunches.

"And this one," Mrs. Bailey said with a hint of distaste, "is for the—*pickpocket.*"

"I'm sure Ganef will appreciate it," Beatrice said, and stowed the two paper bags in the pockets of her jacket.

By this time, Miranda had arrived at the porch steps. Beatrice was pleasantly surprised to see that she was wearing jeans and walking shoes like the rest of them, instead of the beautiful and totally impractical outfits she usually sported. Miranda even smiled as she accepted a sandwich from Mrs. Bailey, without a hint of the arrogance that had always been her trademark. And then Beatrice noticed the chain around Miranda's neck. Hanging from it was a silver pentagram with a small ruby in the center. The ruby was the Bailiwick stone, and Beatrice was wearing an identical charm that Miranda had given her.

"Hi," Miranda said brightly. "I hope I'm not late."

And she's considerate now, too, Beatrice thought. "No, you're right on time," she said.

Miranda Pengilly was even taller than Beatrice and exquisitely beautiful. Her black hair was cut short, like a boy's, and her smoky-lashed eyes were such a pale shade of gray they appeared almost silver. She looked just the same, except the smug smile and bored indifference were gone. Miranda actually looked happy to see them all. And Beatrice was glad to see her cousin. Miranda had been the cause of a lot of worry and aggravation, but she'd turned out to be a brave and loyal friend.

Mr. and Mrs. Bailey greeted Miranda warmly, as did Ollie and Cyrus. Even Teddy smiled at Miranda, and then she asked, "Are you going to be a pain in the neck on this trip, too?"

There was a flicker of the old temper in Miranda's eyes, but instead of responding with a sharp retort, she started to laugh. And then everyone else was laughing, even Teddy.

"I'll *try* to behave myself," Miranda said, grinning, when they'd quieted down, "but you keep an eye on me, Teddy, you hear?"

"Don't think I won't," Teddy murmured.

"We'd better get going," Beatrice said, picking up her backpack.

This was the moment she always dreaded, knowing that her parents' real worry was just beginning. But Mr. and Mrs. Bailey appeared composed, obviously trying hard to make this as easy as possible for their daughter.

"We'll see you when you get back then," Mr. Bailey said, engulfing Beatrice in a big hug.

"And you know not to take any unnecessary risks," Mrs. Bailey said, her voice cracking only a little. She kissed Beatrice's cheek and looked around at the others. "I want all of you to promise to be extra careful this time," she said sternly.

They all assured her that they wouldn't do anything foolish, and then they were off, heading down the street in the direction of the antique shop. A pale ribbon of gold was just beginning to show above the horizon when they reached *Mathias Snow Antiques*.

"I can't believe the Executive Committee wimped out," Miranda said as they crossed the street to the shop. "Don't they know there's always danger when you're dealing with Dally Rumpe?"

"I told them that!" Teddy exclaimed. "They're just more cautious than we are—maybe because they're older."

"Or wiser," Ollie said lightly, but Beatrice could see by his expression that he was serious.

"I still think calling off the test is totally unfair," Teddy said.

"I couldn't agree more," Miranda replied. "But if we break the spell, they'll probably classify us Classical, anyway."

"I think so, too," Teddy said, obviously delighted to have her hopes reinforced.

Beatrice just smiled. Apparently, Teddy had gotten over her jealousy and was becoming fast friends with Miranda. For the moment, anyway. They really were like two peas in a pod.

The sign in the front window of the shop read *Closed*, but when Beatrice tried the door, she found it unlocked. They walked into the dimly lit interior, no one saying a word.

Then Mathias Snow appeared as abruptly as before, still wearing the stained velvet jacket, and said softly, "This way," with a dramatic sweep of his arm.

Miranda's eyebrows lifted as she caught Beatrice's eye. Beatrice just gave a little shrug and hurried after the shop owner, nearly bumping into a life-size sculpture of a grizzly bear.

"Good grief!" Miranda muttered under her breath. "Who would buy any of this junk?"

Mathias Snow led then through the cluttered shop to a doorway in the back wall, and then down a creaky flight of wooden steps lit only by one faint bulb hanging from the ceiling. When he reached the bottom of the staircase, he flipped a switch, and a feeble circle of light appeared in the center of the cellar, but the rest was left in shadow.

They followed him across the uneven dirt floor to a particularly dark corner, and Beatrice glanced around apprehensively. *Where's Ganef?* she wondered, and the idea flashed through her mind that this strange witch might be planning to lock them up and leave them down here. But then a figure stepped out of the shadows, and even in the dim light, there was no mistaking that it was Ganef.

"Merry meet," Ganef said, his cheerful tone reassuring. "Are you ready to leave for Heraldstone?"

"We're ready," Beatrice said.

Ganef and Mathias Snow began to push on the plastered wall in front of them, and a section of the wall opened up with a groan. Beatrice and the others found themselves peering into a dark tunnel.

"You'll let me know when Wolf has more merchandise for me," the shop owner said to Ganef.

"It may be awhile," Ganef replied. "There's not much worth stealing in Heraldstone these days."

"But that could all change," Mathias Snow said in his silky voice, staring at Beatrice.

"We're hoping it will," Ganef said.

No wonder Mathias Snow is helping Wolf, Beatrice thought. *He gets stolen goods from him to sell.*

The shop owner reached for a lantern on the shelf behind him. He lit the candle inside and handed the lantern to Ganef.

"Well, let's get going," the boy said briskly, and stepped through the opening in the wall.

Beatrice and her companions followed Ganef into the tunnel. With the light from the lantern, they could see that it was wide enough for three to walk abreast. Beatrice and Ollie fell into step on either side of Ganef, and the others followed behind.

The walls and floor of the tunnel were packed clay, with wooden braces and beams across the earth ceiling, which was several feet above their heads.

"Does this go all the way to the Sphere?" Beatrice asked.

"All the way to Heraldstone," Ganef replied. Then he glanced back at Miranda. "Who's that?" he asked Beatrice. "Wolf thought there would only be four. He has photos of everyone but her."

"That's my cousin, Miranda Pengilly," Beatrice said. "She was with us on our last two trips to the Sphere. I hope it's all right that we brought her."

Ganef shrugged. "It's all right with me."

Beatrice heard Miranda mutter something and wondered if her cousin had really changed as much as it seemed. Because she thought Miranda had said, *Tough luck, if it isn't.*

49

"So tell us about Heraldstone," Ollie said. "From what Beatrice said, it sounds like a walled medieval city."

Ganef gave Ollie a blank look. "I don't know what that is," he said, "but since you're used to all the modern conveniences in the mortal world, it might seem strange to you. For instance, we don't have water running out of pipes like Mathias Snow has. We draw our water at one of the town wells and carry it home in buckets."

"You're kidding!" Teddy exclaimed. "All the other places we've visited in the Sphere had running water."

"Like I told you," Ganef said, "Heraldstone's been cut off from the rest of the Sphere for more than two hundred years."

"So how do you take showers?" Miranda asked.

"Showers?" The word seemed to baffle Ganef.

"Uh—baths," Teddy said. "How do you bathe?"

"Oh, every few months we heat water over the fire and pour it in a tub," Ganef said. "Then all the men who want to bathe take turns, and the last one dumps the water out the window."

Cyrus snickered. "Every few months?"

"You mean," Teddy said, "you all bathe in the same water?"

"Sure," Ganef said. "Why not?"

Beatrice looked over her shoulder and shot Teddy a warning look. Teddy just rolled her eyes.

For the next two hours, Ganef entertained them with tales of Wolf's illustrious past. He came from a long line of thieves, according to Ganef, the best in the Sphere.

"Why, Wolf's great-great-great-grandfather, Ebenezer Duvall, was even a frequent visitor to Bailiwick Castle,"

Ganef said with a laugh, "in the middle of the night, of course."

"You mean, he robbed Bromwich?" Cyrus asked.

"So I've been told," Ganef said. "The way Wolf tells it, old Ebenezer and Bromwich had a friendly kind of contest going on—with Ebenezer trying to take everything he could, and Bromwich trying to catch him at it. One time, the law stepped in and was going to arrest Ebenezer, and Bromwich told them to mind their own business, that Ebenezer had a right to make a living just like everybody else."

Beatrice laughed, liking this side of Bromwich. Then she thought of him sitting in a cold, damp dungeon, all alone (for two hundred years!), and was stricken with guilt for wishing—even for a moment—that she didn't have to return to the Sphere.

"Can we rest for a few minutes?" Teddy asked.

"Why don't we eat?" Cyrus added. "I'm hungry."

Everyone agreed, and brought out the lunches Mrs. Bailey had fixed for them. Beatrice handed a bag to Ganef.

"What's this?" he asked, holding up a ham-and-cheese sandwich.

Beatrice told him what it was, and he took a big bite. As he chewed, a smile spread across his face. He liked the coconut pie even more.

After lunch, Beatrice placed Cayenne back in her traveling pocket and they started walking again. Ganef continued to tell them tales about the thieves' exploits. A long time later, Ganef fell silent, either because he had run out of stories or was feeling as tired as everyone else. Beatrice's legs were beginning to ache and she was thirsty.

She was about to ask if they could take a few minutes to rest, when she saw a faint light some distance ahead.

"What's that?" she asked Ganef.

"One of Wolf's men, I expect," the boy replied, but Beatrice noticed the sudden tension in his face. "We patrol the tunnel close to Heraldstone."

"But it might *not* be one of Wolf's men?" Ollie asked.

"Chances are, it is," Ganef answered, his tone sharper now, "but stay quiet. We'll know soon."

The boy had become watchful and furtive, as alert as a tiger stalking its prey. As they continued in silence down the tunnel, Beatrice felt goose bumps pop up on her arms. This was the Ganef who had followed her and Teddy, the thief who had grabbed her and pulled a knife as easily as he breathed. The good-natured storytelling Ganef had lulled her into a false feeling of security. But now she had to face reality: They were entering a world like none she had ever known, the dangerous world of outlaws who lived by their wits. Beatrice's heart began to pound, and she was glad when Ollie reached for her hand and squeezed it.

Suddenly, a loud cry echoed through the tunnel, like the warning call of some strange bird. Cyrus yelped and Teddy grabbed Beatrice's arm. Ganef stopped short, but when Beatrice looked at him, expecting to see his knife drawn again, she realized that the boy was smiling.

"It's only Badger," Ganef said, his body relaxing. Then he cupped his hands around his mouth and imitated the cry they had just heard.

"Come on," Ganef said, beginning to walk fast. "Badger is one of Wolf's lookouts. We're almost there."

Badger, it turned out, was a stocky boy about Ganef's age with straw-colored hair and a dirty face. He strode up to Ganef, swinging his lantern and grinning, revealing a few missing teeth.

"So you've brought the powerful witches to us, have you?" Badger said. Then he peered at Beatrice and the others, and grunted. "They don't look like much to me. Why, they're just kids!"

Beatrice felt Teddy bristle beside her. Miranda walked up to Badger, hands on her hips, and said, "This is Wolf's lookout? Surely you're joking, Ganef. *Why, he's just a kid!*"

"Miranda!" Beatrice said sharply. All they needed was to make one of Wolf's thieves mad.

The look of fury that flashed across Badger's face made even Miranda take a step back, but then his expression changed as swiftly as the wind, and the lookout clapped his palms against his thighs and began to laugh. Ganef just stood there, smiling, until finally, Badger wiped his eyes and muttered, "That was a good one."

"Come on," Ganef said. "I've got to take these witches to Wolf."

With Badger walking alongside Ganef, and looking back at Miranda from time to time with an appreciative smirk, they continued along the tunnel until they reached a flight of stone steps. Badger ran ahead, taking the steps two at a time, and pushed open a heavy wooden door, allowing daylight to stream in. As Beatrice climbed the steps, she wondered what in the world awaited them on the other side of that door.

Badger held the door open, and Beatrice and the others followed Ganef out into the sunlight. They emerged at a spot where two narrow cobbled streets intersected. Buildings of plaster or wood, and a few built from stone, rose two and three stories high all around them. Beatrice caught a glimpse of a massive stone wall with wide wooden gates at the end of one of the streets.

"We're *inside* Heraldstone," Beatrice said in surprise.

"That's right," Ganef replied. "That wall you're looking at circles the town, and those are the main gates." Then he grinned. "But Wolf's men have their own entrances, and you've just passed through one of them."

Badger shut the heavy door that led to the tunnel with a great slam and then jerked its handle.

"He's making sure it's locked," Ganef said. "Only Wolf and a few others have keys to open it from this side."

There weren't many people on the streets of Heraldstone. Two women were standing on a doorstep talking and another was sweeping a cloud of dust out her front door. A young man was rolling a keg off a cart and up a ramp into a building, and down the block, an old one was shouting at two small boys, who were running away as fast as their legs would carry them. Beatrice noticed that all the people had one thing in common: Their clothing was old and tattered and resembled styles she had seen in history books. The buildings, the young man's cart and skinny horse—it was as if Beatrice had stepped back into the Middle Ages. But there was nothing terrifying about the place. In fact, Beatrice thought the town of Heraldstone was quaint and interesting.

"Will you be at The Ghost later?" Badger asked Ganef.

"Unless Wolf has something for me to do."

"Then I'll see you there," Badger said, and with a wave, quickly disappeared into an alleyway.

"I'd better be getting you to Wolf," Ganef said to Beatrice, and started down the street.

"What's the ghost Badger was talking about?" Cyrus asked.

"A tavern," Ganef replied. "The Galloping Ghost. It's next door to Wolf's house, so you'll probably want to take your meals there. The rest of us do."

They passed a bakery with bread and pastries displayed in the window, and another shop sporting old-fashioned boots and shoes, but many of the businesses had their windows boarded up. Beatrice tried to take in everything as she hurried after Ganef, who was turning onto streets and cutting through alleys until Beatrice didn't have any idea how far they were from the main gates.

Finally, Ganef stopped at a corner and pointed up to a sign that read: *Robbers' Mile*. "This is Wolf's street," Ganef said. "We aren't far from his house."

"Interesting name," Ollie said as they started after Ganef down Robbers' Mile. "What does it mean?"

"Just what it says," Ganef replied. "The street circles the town, and they say, goes on for a mile—and it's the home of most of Heraldstone's robbers. The ones who admit to it, anyway," he added with a grin.

Just then, a half dozen men stepped out from between two buildings and stopped in front of Ganef. Their faces were as rough and battered as the shirts and trousers they wore, and from the scowls on their faces, Beatrice could only surmise that this meeting had been planned. Then, when the men spread out so that she and her companions couldn't pass, Beatrice was certain of it.

"Look here!" one of the men said. "It's young Ganef. And who does he have with him?"

"You know very well, Pinchgutt," Ganef said, frowning. "Now let us pass. Wolf's expecting us."

Pinchgutt snorted and gave Ganef a scornful look. He was probably no more than thirty, with tangled brown hair falling to his shoulders, a broad nose that made his squinty eyes appear even smaller, and grime embedded in his pores so that his face had a grayish cast to it. He was wearing a brown tunic and trousers and, like Ganef and the others, scuffed leather boots.

"You should show more respect for your elders," Pinchgutt growled. "It's time somebody taught you some manners—even if you *are* Wolf's pet."

Ganef's teeth were clenched so tightly a muscle was twitching along his jawline. "You're just mad because you don't want these witches here," Ganef said, "but Wolf does. And the last I heard, *he's* the one in charge. So back off, Pinchgutt, and take your gripes up with Wolf."

"Wolf, Wolf, Wolf," one of the other men mimicked. "Can't you speak for yourself, Ganef?"

"I just did," Ganef shot back. He pushed through the line of men and beckoned for Beatrice and the others to follow him.

Surprisingly, the thieves let them through. But when Beatrice looked back, a half block or so later, she saw that the men were still standing there, staring after them.

"Wow, that was close," Teddy said softly. "I thought he was going to beat you up, Ganef."

"*I* thought he was going to beat *all of us* up," Cyrus added.

"Nahhh!" Ganef said, but he was still frowning. "Pinchgutt and the others are all right. They're just afraid if you break Dally Rumpe's spell, Heraldstone will become respectable again. They don't want the law moving in. But they won't hurt you—they're too scared of what Wolf would do to them!"

Beatrice didn't have that same confidence in Pinchgutt and his friends. She was still feeling anxious when Ganef stopped abruptly in front of a two-story stone building with a dark red door.

"Well, this is it," the boy said.

The door had a brass knocker shaped like a wolf's head. Ganef knocked three times, paused, and then knocked three times again.

The red door slowly opened.

5

Wolf

A man in black robes was standing in the doorway. He was a curious sight, quite tall and nearly as wide, with a head that was perfectly round and didn't have a single hair on it that Beatrice could see. His eyes glittered like small chips of onyx above fleshy cheeks and jowls that hung down over his collar. From the grim set of his mouth, Beatrice was guessing that he wasn't happy to see them.

She just hoped this wasn't Wolf Duvall, and was relieved when Ganef said, "This is Hobnob, who's been with Wolf longer than anyone. He takes care of the house—and Wolf's visitors, too, when he has any. Wolf's expecting us," he added to Hobnob.

The huge man stepped back so that they could enter, his eyes darting suspiciously from face to face as they crossed the threshold. His unfriendly scrutiny made Beatrice uneasy. When they were all inside, Hobnob turned slowly and started down the hall without a word. Ganef motioned for Beatrice and the others to follow.

The hallway was as wide as a good-size room, with tan stone walls like the exterior of the house. Sconces lined the walls, the candles flickering as they walked past, illuminating old oil portraits and dark landscapes in heavy ornate frames. At the end of the hall were double doors, the ancient wood distressed but polished to a high sheen, and on each side of the doors were long benches upholstered in worn, but still beautiful, silk—a pattern of pale gold stars on a dark red background.

Hobnob stopped at the doors and motioned for them to sit. Beatrice sat down on one of the benches with Ollie and Miranda. Teddy and Cyrus took the bench across from them. But Ganef remained standing.

"I'll be going now," he said to Beatrice. "Wolf doesn't like us hanging around once we've finished a job."

"Thank you for bringing us here," Beatrice said.

"I'm sure you haven't seen the last of me," Ganef said with a grin. "Wolf mentioned that you might need me to show you around."

Hobnob had raised his fist to knock on one of the doors, but now he turned toward Ganef, hand still poised in the air. Beatrice could see disapproval in the look he gave the young pickpocket.

Ganef saw it, too, and began to fidget. "I'm just following Wolf's orders," he mumbled.

"Dally Rumpe has always left the thieves alone," Hobnob said, the deep rumble of his voice startling Beatrice. "All this will do is ignite his wrath. And he'll be most angry with Wolf—for taking them into his house."

Ganef shrugged and started to back away. "Wolf's thought it through," he said stiffly. "It's not up to me to question his decisions."

Then the boy raised his hand in a wave of farewell to Beatrice and her companions and headed for the front door. Beatrice realized suddenly that she had begun to trust Ganef—and she felt vulnerable in this unfamiliar house without him. Hobnob was beyond strange, and certainly didn't give Beatrice warm fuzzies—and Wolf? Even the thought of meeting him made her heart begin to pound.

"Wait here," Hobnob said gruffly, and knocked on the door.

When a man's voice told him to enter, Hobnob went inside and closed the door behind him.

Beatrice had placed her backpack on the floor near her feet. Now she noticed that Cayenne was struggling to get out of her pocket.

"Take it easy, Cay," Beatrice said, and bent down to free the cat.

Cayenne leaped to the stone floor and stretched. Then she stared up at Beatrice, looking out of sorts.

Beatrice picked up the cat and began to stroke her gently. "I know," she said softly. "It's been a long day, Cayenne. For all of us."

Just then, one of the doors opened, and Hobnob motioned abruptly for them to enter. Holding Cayenne close, as much for her own reassurance as for the cat's, Beatrice walked through the door.

It was a big room, obviously a study or library, judging from the shelves of books that covered three of the walls from floor to ceiling. A massive fireplace took up most of the fourth wall, with sculpted animal figures supporting the stone mantle. Beatrice looked closer and saw that the animals were wolves, their features carved with such detail in the pale stone that the creatures looked almost alive. A fire was lit, and dozens of candles in heavy silver holders filled the room with warmth. Beatrice wasn't sure what she had expected a thief's home to look like, but it wasn't this.

Then a man stood up from behind a large desk, and all eyes turned toward him. He was probably in his forties, not especially tall, but his presence dominated the space. His velvet robes were a warm golden brown, and the gleaming hair that fell past his shoulders was nearly the same color, with discreet streaks of silver.

"Please, come in," the man said, his tone commanding, but not rude or threatening. In fact, he had a pleasant voice, and the smile on his lean face seemed genuine.

"I'm Wolf Duvall," he said, "and I know who all of you are—except," he paused, his intelligent brown eyes resting on Miranda, "for you."

"This is my cousin, Miranda Pengilly," Beatrice said. "She's helped us on our last two trips to the Sphere. I hope you don't mind that we brought her."

"Certainly not," Wolf replied. Then his eyebrows drew together thoughtfully. "Pengilly," he murmured, and looked at Miranda again. "Are you, by any chance, related to Donato Pengilly, the writer?"

Miranda looked surprised, then pleased. "He's my grandfather."

"His novels are extraordinary," Wolf said. "I especially liked *The Old Witch and the Sea*. I've read it at least five times."

Then he pointed them to chairs near the fireplace, and told Hobnob, who was lurking in the corner, to bring them cups of witches' brew and a bowl of dragon's milk for Beatrice's cat. Hobnob hesitated for only a second, and then, with his lips pressed tightly together, left the room and closed the door behind him.

Wolf sat down and looked at them, smiling faintly. "Don't take any notice of Hobnob. He's been around so long, he thinks he owns me. And he's a little concerned about me bringing you here."

Beatrice sat back in the upholstered chair, which proved very comfortable, and blew her bangs out of her eyes. "We had gotten that impression," she said. "And there must be others who don't want us here. There always are."

Wolf's smile vanished instantly. Now Beatrice could see irritation in his face, and something else that she couldn't identify. But whatever it was, it was vaguely disturbing.

"Has anyone bothered you?" Wolf asked sharply. "Or said something to frighten you? Because that won't be tolerated."

"No, not at all," Beatrice said hastily.

Wolf's sudden change of mood and manner was unsettling. Beatrice could see that beneath the facade of courtesy and kindness was something hard and ungiving. She could imagine that the punishment for going against his wishes would be harsh and swift. She certainly hoped that he never became angry with *her*.

"Well," Wolf said, his smile returning, "if anyone makes you feel the least bit unwelcome, tell me at once. I want your stay in my home to be as pleasant as possible."

"Thank you for inviting us here," Beatrice said.

Just then, Hobnob came back with a tray bearing six silver goblets and a small silver bowl containing the dragon's milk for Cayenne. Wolf, himself, placed the bowl on the Oriental carpet near his feet. Never one to hesitate where refreshments were involved, Cayenne leaped to the floor and began to lap up the milk greedily.

Watching her, Wolf laughed softly. "I've heard about your cat-familiar, as well. She's been very helpful to you, hasn't she?"

"She's saved my life more than once," Beatrice replied.

After Hobnob had left, Wolf took a sip of his witches' brew, and then he said, "Ganef told me that he explained to you why I'm anxious for you to break the final part of Dally Rumpe's spell. My reasons are strictly economic." He was looking steadily at Beatrice, assessing her. "Dally Rumpe has never bothered us—I imagine he rather likes the idea of a town run by outlaws—but his presence has driven away all the business that used to go on here, and the thieves are suffering along with everyone else."

Beatrice didn't know what to say, so she just nodded.

"My reasons for supporting you aren't lofty ones," Wolf continued, "and you probably have mixed feelings about accepting help from me. You may be asking yourself whether you want to be responsible for Heraldstone getting back on its feet just so a bunch of thieves can line their pockets. But what I do—what any of the town's residents do—isn't your concern, Beatrice. You've come to return Bailiwick to the way it was before Dally Rumpe brought his evil here and to free Bromwich from his prison. And I want to help you do it. It's as simple as that."

Everything he had said was true. Beatrice *did* feel uncomfortable accepting help from thieves, but it was also true that she didn't have any control over what people did

63

once Dally Rumpe's spell was broken. Besides, she and her friends had no other choice that she could see.

"You'll probably need a few days," Wolf said, "to look around and to think about how you're going to enter the castle. With anyone else, I'd say that's going to be impossible, but Ganef told me that he's seen your powers."

Beatrice nearly choked on her witches' brew, and the others shifted uneasily.

Wolf went on as if he hadn't noticed anything. "You may not need any more help from me, but I do have some ideas that might make your job easier. My great-great-great-grandfather, Ebenezer Duvall, used to rob Bromwich's castle regularly—of course, there were no goblins and Furies back then, not even an enchanted bridge, or a moat filled with flesh-eating fish. But he passed down information that might be useful to you. On the other hand," Wolf said, frowning, "I think I should tell you that my great-grandfather, Sam Hill Duvall, tried to break into Dally Rumpe's Treasure Room, where all his gold and precious stones were stored—and I assume, still are—and failed. In fact, my great-grandfather was killed trying."

"I'm sorry," Beatrice murmured.

"So, perhaps I was wrong," Wolf said, staring absently into the fire, "when I said that my reasons for helping you were strictly economic. I, too, have a family score to settle."

"Have you ever tried to enter the castle?" Ollie asked.

Wolf surfaced from wherever his thoughts had taken him, and a grin spread across his face, making him seem younger and more likeable. "I'm not *that* foolish. Nor that brave, either. But you five have managed to outwit Dally

Rumpe over and over," he said, a hint of respect creeping into his voice, "and it's my hope that you can do it again."

Beatrice didn't have time to respond because, at that moment, there came a sharp rapping on the door. Then the door swung open and Hobnob came rushing in—red-faced and obviously alarmed.

Wolf was instantly alert. "What's happened?"

"It's John Chew," Hobnob said. "He's been wounded."

Wolf shot out of his chair and made for the door. Beatrice and the others hurried after him.

A man who looked quite a bit younger than Wolf was lying on one of the upholstered benches in the hall, his elegant blue cape sweeping the floor. In a glance, Beatrice took in the thick fair hair, the closed eyes, the handsome face grimacing with pain—and the front of the fawn-colored vest soaked with blood.

Wolf dropped down beside the injured man. "John," Wolf said urgently, "can you hear me?"

John Chew's eyelids fluttered, then slowly lifted. His eyes were the same sky blue as his cape.

"The castle," he whispered. "Goblins—" Then he groaned and clasped his bloody chest.

Wolf's head swung around to Hobnob. "Do you know where he intended to ride today?"

"Just out to Bailiwick Castle," Hobnob said. "He'd heard two coaches would be passing late morning. He planned to wait out on the plain and see if they were worth holding up."

"But he said something about goblins," Wolf said, turning back to the wounded man. "They must have been from Bailiwick Castle. But that doesn't make sense—

they've never bothered highwaymen out on the plain before."

John Chew raised the hand from his chest, his palm and fingers now covered with blood. "*Were* from the castle," he said haltingly. "Twenty, twenty-five goblins . . . had swords . . . warned me—" He began to cough, and then started gasping for breath.

"Take it easy, my friend," Wolf said quickly, his voice surprisingly gentle.

Then he turned to Hobnob again. "Go get Doc Llewellyn. And tell him to hurry."

Hobnob took off, and Wolf leaned over the highwayman.

"Warned me," John Chew repeated softly.

"Don't try to talk," Wolf said.

The highwayman grabbed hold of Wolf's hand with his bloodied one and looked fiercely into Wolf's eyes. "Everyone's to stay off the plain—and clear of the castle."

"We're no longer allowed on the plain?" Wolf asked, looking puzzled.

John Chew nodded weakly. "Goblins said . . . anyone near the castle . . . chopped into little pieces." Then, breathing hard from the exertion of talking, he closed his eyes again.

Wolf looked up at Beatrice. "They've never attacked us before," he said grimly. "I must have been right then. Dally Rumpe is feeling backed into a corner. He'll go after anyone who comes near the castle—and that includes you, Beatrice—I'd say, *especially* you."

6

Pinchgutt's Warning

Hobnob was back very soon with a thin, dour-looking man in tan robes. The scant amount of hair he had was the same washed-out color as his pasty face, and did little to cover his bony dome. Like most of the thieves Beatrice had seen in Heraldstone, Doc Llewellyn looked none too clean. There was even dirt under his fingernails!

Beatrice couldn't believe the man was really a doctor. But Wolf seemed glad to see him, and he moved away from John Chew so that the physician could kneel down and take care of his patient.

"Show our guests to their rooms," Wolf said to Hobnob. "You'll probably want to rest after your trip," he added to Beatrice. "When you're hungry, you can go next door to the tavern. The owner will put all your meals on my tab."

Beatrice and the others thanked him, but Wolf had already turned back to watch Doc Llewellyn examine John Chew's wounds. As Hobnob led them down the hall toward a staircase, Beatrice could hear Wolf asking the doctor, "Is it as bad as it looks, Archibald? The sword must have missed his heart or he'd be lying dead out on the plain. But he seems to have lost a lot of blood."

"Give me a minute," Doc Llewellyn murmured. "There's just the one wound—but it's deep. Why do you think they did this, Wolf? They've never attacked any of your men before."

Beatrice was too far away now to hear Wolf's answer. She and her companions followed the lumbering Hobnob up the steep, creaky stairs, and then down a hall with rough plaster walls and only the occasional candle sconce to light it. They passed two closed doors, one on either side of the corridor, and then Hobnob stopped at the third and fourth doors. He opened one of them, and Cayenne ran inside.

"I'll have a servant bring you water and towels," Hobnob said, sounding as if it hurt him to be the least bit courteous. He opened the door across the hall and looked in the general direction of Ollie and Cyrus. "You gentlemen will be in this room."

Beatrice, Teddy, and Miranda followed Cayenne into a long, narrow room that had four cotlike beds lined up in a row. At the end of the room was a washstand with a large ironstone bowl, a straight-back chair, and a three-drawer chest. The only decoration anywhere was an old spotted mirror hanging over the washstand.

Miranda shut the door and looked around. "Simplicity itself," she said. "There isn't even a closet."

"Or a bathroom," Teddy added. She pointed to a curtain strung on wire in the corner. "Maybe that's the closet," she said, pulling back the curtain. Then she gave a short laugh. "Nope! But I found the bathroom—which consists of one chamber pot. I think that's what you call it."

"*Come on*," Miranda muttered. "This is positively primitive!"

"Well, at least the beds look clean," Beatrice said, noting that each was made up with crisp white sheets and had a gray blanket folded at the foot.

"But they're so narrow," Teddy said. "I'll probably roll out onto the floor."

Miranda sat down on the first bed and rubbed her hand across the rough wool blanket. "These must have been made from scouring pads."

Beatrice was growing impatient. "Get over it, both of you," she said briskly. "This isn't a resort hotel, you know. And when you think about it, it's not so bad for a thief's digs."

Cayenne had curled up on one of the beds and was already snoring loudly.

"See," Beatrice said, hoisting her backpack onto the bed next to her cat's, "Cayenne isn't complaining, and she's even more spoiled than the two of you."

"I *resent* that," Miranda muttered.

There was a knock on the door, and then Ollie and Cyrus stuck their heads in.

"Are your accommodations as luxurious as ours?" Teddy asked the boys.

"Not quite," Ollie answered with a grin. "Your pillows are fluffier than ours."

"It sure is cold in here," Cyrus said, shivering a little even though he was still wearing his jacket.

"I noticed that," Beatrice said. "Obviously there's no central heat—and not even a fireplace. I wonder how they heat these rooms."

"They don't," Miranda said flatly. "I think we'll be sleeping in our clothes."

Ollie sat down on the bed beside Cayenne and stroked the cat absently, his expression thoughtful. "You know, that highwayman, John Chew, was badly hurt. Dally Rumpe isn't beating around the bush this time, is he?"

"What if we can't get inside the castle?" Cyrus asked.

"We'll get in," Miranda said firmly, and then added with less conviction, "somehow."

"So what do you think of Wolf?" Ollie asked, looking at Beatrice.

"He seems nice enough," Beatrice replied, frowning as she thought about their host, "but did you see how mad he got when he thought someone might have made us feel unwelcome? I wouldn't want to cross him."

"Well, *I* don't think he's telling us everything," Miranda said. "I don't trust him at all."

"Neither do I," Beatrice admitted, and the others nodded.

"There aren't any locks on the doors," Teddy pointed out. "Do you think we're safe here?"

"We'll have to stay alert," Ollie replied.

Just then, there was another knock on the door. Beatrice jumped—*This place is making me skittish*, she thought—and expecting to see Hobnob, she yelled, "Come in!"

But this time, it was a very small man who entered the room, carrying a pitcher in one hand and holding a stack of white towels against his chest with the other. Beatrice took one look at him and thought, *Gosh, he's ugly*. Then she felt ashamed. But he *was* one of the most unattractive people she had ever seen.

"I'm Ludwig," the man said, his words coming out like a growl.

He was no more than three feet tall, with a scrawny body and a gnarled little face that reminded Beatrice of a dried-up apple. His dark hair seemed to sprout in all directions, and his eyes were mere dots on either side of a long, pointed nose. His mouth was a thin-lipped gash that appeared to be set in a permanent scowl. Wolf must have provided the neat blue jacket and matching trousers, but Ludwig's long feet—with nails that curved under like claws—were bare.

Ludwig stomped back to the washstand and tossed the towels into an untidy heap beside the ironstone bowl. Then he slammed the pitcher down beside them, sloshing water on the towels.

Beatrice and the others watched him in fascination.

"What are you staring at?" Ludwig demanded suddenly, glaring over his shoulder at them. "Haven't you ever seen a spriggan before?"

"Actually," Ollie said, "we haven't."

"What's a spriggan?" Cyrus asked.

Ludwig's eyes rolled skyward and he scowled more fiercely. "Now I have to educate them, too?" he muttered. Then he spun around and said with the utmost irritation, "Spriggans are clever and ugly and totally unpleasant. We're best known for stealing peoples' children and creating whirlwinds to destroy crops."

"There don't seem to *be* any crops around here," Ollie said.

"Of course there aren't, you ignoramus!" Ludwig was tapping one long bare foot on the floor, looking ready to explode. "I don't live with the spriggans anymore! My parents left me in this witch town when I was quite young."

"Why?" Teddy wanted to know.

"Because I was ugly and mean," Ludwig snapped, "even by spriggan standards. They crept into town in the middle of the night and left me on a doorstep. But no one wanted a spriggan baby, so Wolf offered to take me. When I was old enough, he gave me a job. Now are you satisfied, you nosy brats?"

Beatrice felt her face growing warm, but she managed to say in a relatively polite voice, "That was a kind thing for Wolf to do."

"Kind, right," Ludwig muttered, looking more annoyed than ever. "But spriggans aren't meant to be cooped up in houses. We're supposed to live in the wild, preferably in dark, damp mounds of earth. I've never known a spriggan who was a servant. Housework isn't in our blood!"

Just then, they heard shouts and laughter from outside. Beatrice and the others moved to the window and saw a group of rough-looking men gathered on the street below. It was the six thieves who had tried to bar their way when they were with Ganef. The one called Pinchgutt peered up at the window, and when he saw them standing there, a nasty grin spread across his grimy face. There was something threatening in the way he looked at them, and Beatrice felt a shiver dart down her spine.

"Some of Wolf's men," Ludwig said with disdain. "Uncouth louts! They have quarters in the cellar, but they're always traipsing into the house—and *I* have to mop up the dirt they track in. I could steal just as well as them—no, *better!*—but Wolf says he has more thieves than he needs—it's house help that's scarce."

Beatrice glanced at the unhappy little man, and said, "If you don't like your life here, why don't you leave?"

"*And go where?*" he screeched. Then he muttered, "Besides, there *are* benefits to working for Wolf."

When Ludwig finally stomped out of the room, slamming the door behind him, Cyrus said, "I'm hungry."

"Why don't we wash up and check out the tavern?" Ollie suggested.

A few minutes later, they came downstairs, with Cayenne perched on Beatrice's shoulder. There was no sign of Wolf or anyone else. Beatrice looked down the hall and saw that John Chew had been taken away.

They stepped outside into the bright, chilly afternoon and headed for the building next door. A sign creaking in the wind read: *The Galloping Ghost*. As they approached the tavern, Beatrice saw someone standing in the doorway. It was Pinchgutt.

"I knew you'd have to eat sooner or later," the thief said.

Beatrice didn't like the feeling that she was being stalked, and at the moment, she felt more exasperated with the man than frightened by him.

"Why are you following us?" she asked curtly. "If it's to tell us to get lost—"

"Just wait a minute, young witch," Pinchgutt interrupted, holding up his hands to silence her. "I'm here to give you a piece of information—and it's for your own good."

Now that they were face-to-face, there was nothing particularly threatening about the thief. He just looked very serious and a bit irritated by her verbal assault.

Miranda had stepped forward to stand beside Beatrice. "All right," she said sharply, "what's the information?"

Pinchgutt's expression turned sullen. He seemed to like Miranda's tone even less than Beatrice's.

"What I have to say is this," the thief answered, giving Miranda a withering look before turning his attention back to Beatrice. "It may seem like Wolf Duvall is doing you a favor, but he's out for himself. *Always.* If he saw a way to make a profit by turning you over to Dally Rumpe, he'd do it in a second—and not lose any sleep over it. So that's what I had to tell you, Beatrice Bailiwick. *Don't trust Wolf!*"

"Why are you telling us this?" Ollie asked. "I thought you worked for Wolf."

"I do," Pinchgutt said, "and have for a long time. That's how I've come to know what drives him—and that's silver and gold. And the reason why I don't feel the least bit bad talking about him this way," the thief went on, "is—well, let's just say that I'm fed up with doing all the work and him getting most of the profits. He takes just about everything we bring in—and bribes us to tell if we know of anyone holding out on him."

Beatrice wondered if Pinchgutt had tried keeping more than his share and been punished for it. But surely

74

Wolf must know that Pinchgutt didn't feel any loyalty to him. Beatrice was pretty certain that not much got past Wolf. So why did he keep Pinchgutt around?

As if he had guessed her thoughts, the thief gave Beatrice a cocky grin and said, "Wolf doesn't want to admit it, but he *needs* me. I can do something that comes in very handy for a thief—something that none of Wolf's other men can do."

"What is it?" Beatrice asked.

"I can walk through walls," Pinchgutt said.

7

The Galloping Ghost

Now that Pinchgutt had had his say, he turned abruptly to go back inside the tavern. Then he stopped, and in a surprisingly gallant move, held the door open for them.

Beatrice and her companions walked into a large room that was dim and smoky and filled with the odors of cooking and unwashed bodies. Long trestle tables were crammed close together, most of them already filled with men whose voices were as rough as their appearance. At a glance, Beatrice surmised that most, if not all, were thieves and other sorts who didn't believe in soap and water. Nor in speaking below a shout. The din created by their conversation and laughter made Beatrice's ears throb. She thought about trying to find another place to eat, but Ganef had said that most of the taverns had closed long ago, and Beatrice supposed that any they would find in Heraldstone wouldn't be very different from The Galloping Ghost.

"There's a table," Ollie shouted, pointing to the other side of the room.

As they made their way through the tangle of tables, the noise lessened. Men stopped talking midsentence to twist around and stare at the new arrivals. By the time Beatrice and her companions were seated, the only sounds in the room were the crackling of the flames in the huge fireplace and the clatter of pots from the kitchen.

Beatrice placed Cayenne on the bench beside her and looked around at the many faces turned in their direction. "They don't seem exactly pleased to see us," she murmured.

"Who cares?" Miranda said with a scowl. "At least they've shut up."

Just then, Beatrice noticed a tall, full-figured woman weaving her way through the tables toward them. She had a white apron tied over her green robes, and bright red curls poked out from under the ruffled cap on her head.

"What an honor!" the woman boomed as she approached their table. "You must be Beatrice Bailiwick and her friends—of course you are! Who else *would* you be?" She flashed them a dazzling smile, her green eyes lively and shrewd as they leaped from one face to another. "I'm Lovie Fitzsimmons, proprietor of The Galloping Ghost. Wolf said to watch out for you and to give you the best of everything."

The men around them had started talking again. But their voices were no more than a low rumble, and they were still watching Beatrice's table intently.

"*Hey!*" came a sudden shout from the crowd. "We don't need you here, Beatrice Bailiwick! Go back where you came from."

Lovie Fitzsimmons spun around, surprisingly quick for a woman of her size, her eyes shooting off green sparks. "And *you* just shut your trap, Bibby Sykes!" she bellowed.

77

"Or I'll be telling Wolf you've been less than warm and welcoming to his guests."

Beatrice heard a grumble from the sea of diners, but she noticed that a lot of the men had suddenly become interested in their food again and were no longer looking this way. Apparently, either they didn't want to tangle with Lovie Fitzsimmons, or her threat of telling Wolf had brought them into line.

"Now, then," Lovie said, turning back to Beatrice's table and giving them her radiant smile again, "we have eel stew and acorn bread. I can toast some nice nettle cheese on your bread, if you like. And will you all be having a mug of witches' brew?"

"I don't suppose," Cyrus said politely, "that you have hamburgers or hot dogs." Cyrus had never been fond of traditional witch food.

"Hot *dog*?" Lovie asked, appearing perplexed and vaguely horrified. "I'm afraid we don't serve dog here—or cat, either." She gave Cayenne an apologetic look. "All we've got today is eel."

"It sounds wonderful," Beatrice said quickly, trying to cover up Teddy and Miranda's snickers. "Everyone will have eel stew."

"And why don't we try the nettle cheese?" Ollie suggested heartily. "And definitely some witches' brew."

"Eel stew, acorn bread with cheese, and witches' brew all around," Lovie said, stealing a suspicious glance at Cyrus. "And what about some eel in dragon's milk for your kitty?"

"Perfect!" Beatrice exclaimed.

Lovie hurried away toward the kitchen, and the air began to vibrate with loud conversation again. Beatrice saw Ganef and Badger sitting at a table with some other boys, and Ganef grinned and waved at her. Pinchgutt was with a group of men as tattered and dirty as himself. The thief was leaning forward intently, elbows on the table, talking nonstop about something that, judging from his expression, must have been very serious. He was so absorbed, he didn't seem to notice Beatrice watching him.

"Hey," Ollie said softly, "look who's just arrived."

Beatrice turned to the door and saw Doc Llewellyn enter the tavern. The physician glanced around the room, saw Beatrice and her companions, and started toward them.

"He's coming over here," Teddy said.

"Good," Beatrice replied. "We can ask him how John Chew is doing."

They greeted the doctor when he arrived at the table, and he murmured "Merry meet" in return, his solemn pasty face never changing expression.

"I wonder if I might join you," Doc Llewellyn said hesitantly. "There doesn't seem to be another vacant seat."

They answered, "Certainly" and "Of course."

The physician sank down on the end of the bench beside Beatrice and across from Ollie. Beatrice noticed the pouches under his eyes and thought he looked exhausted.

"We were at Wolf's when you came to see about John Chew," she said.

"I saw you," Doc Llewellyn replied without much interest.

Then he raised his hand to Lovie as she came bustling out from the kitchen. The tavern owner smiled and nodded and headed back to the kitchen.

"How *is* John Chew?" Ollie asked.

"He'll live," the physician said. "But if that wound had been an inch higher, it would have been a different story."

"Are you the only doctor in Heraldstone?" Miranda asked.

"The only one deranged enough to stay," Doc Llewellyn replied. The corners of his mouth lifted ever so slightly to acknowledge his little joke, and then fell back into place so that his face was as blank as before.

"You must be awfully busy," Beatrice said.

"There's always a busted head or a knife wound to treat," the physician agreed. "Occupational hazards, you know."

Beatrice noticed again the buildup of dirt under his nails and wondered how many of his patients had died from infections. But at least he didn't make his living by robbing people! Filthy or not, he did try to help.

A sudden crash nearby caused everyone at Beatrice's table to jump. Looking around, Beatrice saw the wispy figure of a young man flying through the air, balancing a large empty tray with one hand and laughing his head off. Beatrice had seen ghosts before on her trips to the Sphere, but none that seemed as full of life as this one.

Pewter plates that had obviously been on the ghost's tray now lay on the floor around a table of thieves, all of whom were cursing and shaking food from their hair. The ghost continued to fly around the room, braying with laughter like a donkey.

Doc Llewellyn sighed. "That's Folly," he said, "the phantom for whom The Galloping Ghost was named. In life, his name was Ben Folly, but no one bothers with the Ben anymore. He was killed nearly three hundred years ago, in a brawl in this very tavern, and he refuses to leave."

"Is he always so—high-spirited?" Beatrice asked.

"Oh, this is nothing," the doctor said. "Yesterday he dumped a whole pot of boiling gopher gravy on a customer's head. Burned the poor fellow's eyebrows right off."

Beatrice watched as two thieves chased Folly around the room, screaming at him in fury. "He must be a trial for Lovie," she said.

"Since she can't get rid of him," Doc Llewellyn replied, "she's trying to reform him by giving him work to do. But he can't wash dishes because he just tosses them out the back door, and he can't cook because he always adds some extra ingredient—a cup of hot pepper, a pound of bitter weed, that sort of thing. And obviously," the physician added with a shake of his head, "he can't wait tables, either."

Folly had flown behind the bar and was now throwing large pewter tankards at nearby diners. One hit a man on the temple, and he fell unconscious to the floor.

"Oh, dear," Doc Llewellyn murmured. "Excuse me."

The doctor rose wearily from the table and began to elbow his way through the crowd to the injured man.

Lovie came out of the kitchen carrying a tray filled with plates, bowls, and mugs. She took one look at Folly, who was now throwing loaves of black bread at everyone and laughing like a hyena, and screamed for him to stop immediately. Folly just stuck his tongue out at her and moved on to throwing spoons.

"If he weren't already dead, I'd kill him," Lovie muttered, dropping a bowl and a plate in front of Beatrice with an angry thump.

Beatrice peered at the glistening gray chunks swimming in oily liquid in her bowl—eel stew, presumably—and the hunk of dark bread on her plate that looked as hard as concrete beneath its coating of runny yellow cheese—cheese peppered with *thousands* of nettles—and thought she just might skip one meal. But beside her, Cayenne was already tearing into her bowl of milk-soaked eel with gusto.

Lovie screamed at Folly a few more times, and finally, the ghost circled the room like a chortling tornado and then flew into the kitchen.

The tavern owner turned back to Beatrice. "As if a clientele of outlaws wasn't bad enough," she muttered. But then she caught herself and added hastily, "Not that all of the men are bad. Take Wolf, for instance. He's a real gentleman, and has a good heart, too. He took in that awful Ludwig when no one else would, and he gives the young orphans a place to stay—and when his men get too doddery to be of any use, instead of kicking them out the door, he sees that they live out their days in comfort."

"I didn't know robbers provided retirement plans," Miranda said.

Lovie caught the amusement in Miranda's voice and frowned. "Wolf's a decent man, for all his thieving," she said sharply. "Why, I'd trust Wolf with my life!"

A tall man wearing black trousers and a red brocade vest under a black velvet cape had walked up behind Lovie.

"Don't lay it on too thick, Lovie darling," the man said with a smile. "Wolf is hardly a saint. But I'll never convince you of that, will I? I've always suspected that you were sweet on him."

Lovie's plump faced turned crimson. She hit the man on the arm with her fist, and then said to Beatrice and her companions, "This handsome rogue is Bartholomew Jones, but he's called Blacksheep"—Lovie was beginning to grin, in spite of herself—"because his old, moneyed witch family disinherited him when he turned highway-man."

Blacksheep Jones was still smiling pleasantly, and with his wavy black hair and aristocratic features, Beatrice thought that he was, indeed, a handsome man. Quite elegant, as well, in his lace-trimmed shirt and shining black boots. And to top it off, he was holding a black hat with a red plume attached to the band. Beatrice's eyes dropped to his hands—which actually looked clean!—and she noticed the jeweled rings that adorned several of his long, tapered fingers. He looked every inch the refined and debonair highwayman.

"Blacksheep would have you think he's the best to ever ride the roads," Lovie went on playfully, "and even *I* can't dispute the truth of that. In his youth, he was as sly as a fox and twice as quick."

Blacksheep's eyebrows had lifted and he was staring at Lovie in mock dismay. "In my *youth?*" he repeated. "I'm hardly an old man *yet.*"

"Old for your profession," the tavern owner shot back merrily. "Not many highwaymen make it past thirty-five, and you won't be seeing forty again, my friend. Those silver hairs at your temples attest to that."

Blacksheep pressed his lips together in a sign of pique and looked away.

"In any case, you're my hero," Lovie said quickly, apparently realizing that she had struck a nerve.

Blacksheep's gaze shifted back to her face. "And you are the love of my life," he responded, smiling slightly. "If you keep toying with us, dear Lovie, I'm afraid that Wolf and I will be forced to fight a duel over you."

"Pish-pash!" Lovie exclaimed, suddenly looking quite serious. "And wouldn't that be a waste of time for both of you. I'll not have a man who's a robber and a rogue, no matter *how* handsome he is."

"But I thought you said Wolf is a decent man," Blacksheep Jones said, teasing her.

"So he is. But as long as he continues to steal," Lovie said with finality, "he can duel with you over somebody else."

Beatrice had been listening to their exchange with interest, hardly realizing that she was eating the eel stew and acorn bread, and that neither tasted quite as awful as they looked. Now, Blacksheep Jones turned his eyes on Beatrice and studied her with such intensity that she nearly choked trying to swallow the piece of hard bread in her mouth.

"There are people who don't want you here," the highwayman said to Beatrice, "but I'm not one of them."

"Do you work for Wolf?" Beatrice asked.

Blacksheep Jones frowned. "Hardly! I suppose you'd say that Wolf Duvall and I are friendly rivals. But I respect him for going after what he wants—and I respect the five of you for the same reason. Perhaps," he said suddenly, "I could take you out on the plain to see Bailiwick Castle. If you haven't been there yet."

"No, we haven't," Beatrice said quickly, the blood beginning to pump faster through her veins. "But have you heard about the other highwayman who was injured this morning?"

Blacksheep Jones nodded. "John Chew—a good man. I'm glad to hear he's going to make it. But we won't go close enough to risk attack by the goblins."

"That plain is Blacksheep's playground," Lovie said, eyeing the man fondly. "He'll keep you safe."

"Of course, we'll go!" Teddy exclaimed, her eyes dancing with excitement.

"After lunch then?" the highwayman asked. "I'll meet you out front in half an hour. And if I were you," he added with a grin, "I wouldn't give that cat any more eel. She's about to explode."

Beatrice glanced at Cayenne, and was taken aback when she saw that the cat's front paws were clamped around Cyrus's bowl as she attacked the last bit of his eel stew. Her own bowl was licked clean, and her sides were bulging.

"Cayenne, what am I going to do with you?" Beatrice grumbled.

The cat gulped down the final bite of stew and then waddled across the table to Beatrice, looking drowsy and content.

"A little eel stew never hurt anybody," Lovie said, and added to Cyrus, "but you'll need another bowlful."

She hurried off to get it before a protesting Cyrus could stop her.

8

Bailiwick Castle

When they met Blacksheep Jones outside The Galloping Ghost, he said, "Come on, we'll get you some horses."

A short distance down the winding street was a stable. A lanky stable boy hurried out to greet Blacksheep, calling him Mr. Jones, sir, and Beatrice could see the admiration in his eyes. Slipping him a coin, Blacksheep Jones asked the boy to bring out his horse and five others for his friends, and the boy sped away to do his bidding.

The highwayman's horse was a large black stallion named Appollinaris. Beatrice had never seen such a beautiful animal. But as the stable boy tried to lead him out into the yard, the horse jerked his head back and reared up. He looked like he'd be a handful—until Blacksheep Jones walked up to the animal and whispered something into his ear. Instantly, the stallion became as docile as a drowsy kitten.

Beatrice and the others mounted their own horses, all considerably less impressive than Appollinaris, and once Cayenne was settled at the front of Beatrice's saddle, they followed the highwayman out of the stable yard. He led them through a tangle of cobbled streets and dark alleys until they reached a large open square.

There had been so few people on the streets of Heraldstone that Beatrice was surprised by the crowd gathered here. Merchants' stalls lined the square, and they seemed to be doing a healthy business. Beatrice saw all kinds of witches browsing and buying: young and old, male and female, some in luxurious silk robes and others in the most ragged apparel.

"What is all this?" Beatrice asked Blacksheep.

"It's market day," the highwayman answered, showing no interest in the wares displayed for sale. "Once a week, merchants sell their goods in the square for a pittance. But better to take home a few pennies than none at all."

Beatrice looked into every stall they passed, fascinated by the merchandise. There were bolts of cloth in every color, from the dullest brown to the most brilliant shade of peacock blue. One merchant sold nothing but knives, another cooking pots and utensils. Cayenne caught sight of a stall filled with dozens of small caged birds and emitted a strangled cry.

"Don't even think about it," Beatrice said firmly, clutching the cat to prevent her from making a leap at the birds.

"Look at the jewelry," Miranda said, twisting her head around for one last look at the table covered with glittering rings and necklaces.

"And the leather goods," Teddy said, peering wistfully at a pair of soft knee-length boots.

"And the cakes," Cyrus said, sighing as the aroma from a pastry table reached his nostrils.

"You'll have time to shop when we get back," Blacksheep Jones said. "The merchants are here until dark."

They had left the square behind and were approaching the town gates. Two little boys ran to open the gates for Blacksheep, and he tossed each of them a silver coin. The boys grinned and took off in the direction of the square as the highwayman and his party passed through the gates.

Once outside Heraldstone's walls, Beatrice could see nothing but gently rolling hills and tall grass dancing in the wind. A packed-earth road about six feet wide wound over and around the hills until it disappeared on the horizon.

"How far to the castle?" Ollie asked Blacksheep.

"It's just a short ride," the highwayman answered, and nudged Appolinaris into a trot.

They had gone about a mile, and were climbing the second hill, when Beatrice saw the top of a gray stone tower in the distance.

"Is that Bailiwick Castle?" she asked, feeling suddenly breathless with excitement—and, perhaps, a little fear, as well.

"That's it," Blacksheep Jones replied. "What you're seeing is one of the wall towers. Soon you'll have a view of the entire castle."

As they followed the road up the hill, a high stone wall and another tower came into sight. When they reached the top of the hill, Blacksheep Jones told them to stop. Looking out across the plain with its blowing grasses, Beatrice could see the castle some distance away. Its gray walls formed an enormous square, and at each corner was a tall tower with narrow slits for windows.

"Look there," Blacksheep said grimly. "The goblins on the battlements."

Beatrice hadn't noticed any goblins—and she didn't know what a battlement was—but when she looked more closely, she could see many tiny heads barely showing above the castle walls.

"There's a catwalk on the inside of the wall," Blacksheep told them. "The goblins can walk on it all the way around the castle, keeping an eye out for intruders while still being protected by the wall."

"There must be hundreds of them," Miranda said softly.

"The road isn't even that close to the castle," Ollie observed, "so they had to go out of their way to attack John Chew."

"How are we ever going to manage to get inside?" Cyrus asked in a small voice.

Then Beatrice's eyes were drawn to the tallest tower, which was set well within the castle walls. A black flag was flying atop the tower's peaked roof. It had a gold design on it that Beatrice couldn't make out.

"What kind of flag is that?" she asked.

"It's Dally Rumpe's official flag," Blacksheep replied. "Gold daggers dripping blood on a black background. If you're successful in breaking the last part of his spell," the highwayman went on, giving Beatrice a doubtful look, "they'll hoist a ruby-colored flag with a white winged horse in the center. Ruby red and white—the Bailiwick colors."

"Do you have any idea how we can get inside?" Ollie asked Blacksheep.

"I know this plain," he said, "and where to hide along the road to wait for passing coaches—but no one knows much about the castle. I suppose you've heard about the shaking bridge and the flesh-eating fish in the moat?"

"Yes," Beatrice replied, "but Cyrus can cast a shrinking spell, and I was thinking, if we were very small and light, we might be able to cross without the bridge detecting us."

"But the goblins would see us approach the castle," Teddy protested.

"Maybe not," Ollie said thoughtfully. "If Cyrus shrinks us, the tall grass would act as a screen until we reach the bridge. But it might be hard to walk through grass that high."

They all turned to look at the highwayman, still hoping for a suggestion that hadn't occurred to them. But Blacksheep Jones just shook his head. He removed the hat with the jaunty scarlet plume and stared for a long time at the castle.

Finally, he said, "I don't have any idea how you're going to do it."

They rode back to Heraldstone in silence. When they reached the market in the square, Blacksheep said, "Why don't you do your shopping now? I'll take the horses back to the stable."

Beatrice slid out of the saddle and handed her reins to the highwayman.

"Thanks for taking the time to show us the castle," she said.

"I wasn't much help, I'm afraid," Blacksheep responded. "But I'll keep thinking about it, and maybe I'll come up with something."

They watched him ride slowly down the cobbled street, sitting straight and tall in the saddle, leading the other horses behind him. When he was out of sight, they walked over to the nearest stall.

They were looking at leather boots and belts when a woman in worn brown robes came up to them, smiling shyly.

"I couldn't help noticing that you aren't from around here," the woman said, glancing down at their jeans and walking shoes. "What part of the Sphere are you from?"

"Can't you see they're not *from* the Sphere?" another woman demanded. "Just look at them! They must have come from another *world!*"

That's certainly the truth, Beatrice thought. Then she noticed that almost everyone in the square was staring at them and whispering, their faces suspicious, and some frightened. Even the woman who had been brave enough to ask where they were from had edged away and was watching them anxiously.

"They don't have any contact with the outside world," Ollie whispered to Beatrice, "so anyone who seems different alarms them."

"Do you think they're going to attack us?" Teddy asked.

"No chance," Miranda answered. "See how timid they are?" She frowned, looking angry. "They've been turned into a bunch of scared rabbits. And it's all Dally Rumpe's fault!"

Shopping didn't seem like such a good idea anymore, but Teddy insisted that they stop at the jewelry stall before they left. Everyone quickly selected gifts to take back home to their families. For her mother, Beatrice chose a music box that would play any song she requested, and for her father, a key chain that screamed its location when a careless owner misplaced it. Then she saw the silver charm that looked like Bailiwick Castle. There was even a flag flying from the tallest tower—with a tiny ruby at its center—and inside the castle walls was a minuscule winged horse made from ivory. *Ruby red and white, the Bailiwick colors*, Blacksheep Jones had said. The charm was certainly meant to be Bromwich's castle, and Beatrice would have loved to buy it. But when she checked the price tag, and made a mental conversion from witch money to mortal dollars, she knew she couldn't afford it. Even if the seller had been willing to lower the price a lot!

There was some reluctance on the part of the merchant to accept mortal money for their purchases, but when Ollie told him they were guests of Wolf Duvall's, the old man's attitude changed.

"You're staying with Wolf?" he asked brightly. "Oh, that's all right then. He'll change this paper into silver for me."

They were leaving the market when Teddy pointed out Ganef and Badger on the other side of the square. The boys were lurking behind a stall where candles were sold, grinning, and by all appearances, up to no good.

Beatrice and her companions watched as Badger moved stealthily to the front of the stall. He waited until the candle merchant was busy with a customer, and then pointed his index finger at a counter stacked high with candles.

"I think he's casting a spell," Beatrice said.

The words were barely out of her mouth when an explosion came from the candle stall, then another. Startled by the noise, witches in the square looked around to see what had happened. The explosions continued, even as Badger and Ganef sprinted, laughing, for the nearest alley. The candle merchant was running around in circles outside his stall, screeching, while smoke billowed out into the square.

"It's the candles!" Ollie exclaimed. "They're blowing up like firecrackers."

The explosions finally stopped, and the smoke began to clear. But Beatrice could see that the candle stall was a mess, with globs of blackened wax sticking to the walls and the ceiling, and even to the sides of adjacent stalls.

"That was a foolish thing to do," Ollie said, clearly disapproving of the boys' prank. "Someone could have been hurt. Plus, they've ruined that man's candles."

"But it's an interesting talent," Miranda observed. Being low on magical ability herself, she was always quick to admire—and, regrettably, to envy—such skill in others.

"I wonder if Badger can blow up *anything*," Beatrice said thoughtfully as they left the square.

Twilight came quickly to Heraldstone. Beatrice and her friends had to ask directions twice before they found Robbers' Mile, and it was nearly dark when they finally arrived at Wolf's house. Ollie was just raising his hand to use the wolf door knocker when the red door swung open. But it wasn't Hobnob waiting to let them in; it was Wolf himself.

"So how was your first day in Heraldstone?" he asked. His voice was pleasant enough, but the intensity in his eyes as he looked at them aroused Beatrice's suspicions.

"Fine," she said, lifting the bag that held her purchases. "We went shopping."

"I'm sure the town merchants appreciate the support," Wolf said lightly, smiling. "And did you enjoy your trip to Bailiwick Castle?"

Beatrice was startled. *How did he know?* Obviously, he had someone watching them. But who? And why? Beatrice wasn't sure why she hadn't told him up front about Blacksheep Jones taking them to see the castle. Maybe because she hadn't quite trusted Wolf. And, apparently, she had good reason not to.

"We couldn't see much," Beatrice said, trying to keep her tone casual, even though her heart was beating a mile a minute.

"Just the walls," Ollie added.

"And Dally Rumpe's flag," Teddy said.

"And all those goblins!" Cyrus exclaimed.

His friends glanced at him, their message clear: *You're saying too much*, and Cyrus ducked his head.

"It would appear," Wolf said, his tone suddenly chilly, "that you saw quite a lot."

After Wolf had returned to his study and closed the door, Beatrice and the others started down the hall toward the staircase.

"So who told him?" Miranda demanded.

"Anyone in this town could be his spy," Ollie answered softly.

They passed by a small door under the stairs, and Beatrice stopped short. She had noticed a piece of blue cloth sticking out between the door and its frame. The others looked at her inquiringly, and Beatrice quickly put her finger to her lips. Then she walked over to the door, turned the knob, and jerked the door open.

Behind the door was a closet, filled with brooms and mops—and Ludwig!

When the spriggan saw them all standing there, his jaw dropped and his tiny eyes opened as wide as possible. He was clearly shocked that they had found him, and totally unaware that the tail of his jacket caught in the door had given him away.

But Ludwig recovered quickly. In about two seconds he was stomping out of the closet and down the hall, muttering that a person couldn't have *any* privacy with all these strangers in the house.

"He was hiding in there to spy on us," Teddy said with certainty.

Ollie nodded. "I thought I heard a door creak when we were talking to Wolf. It must have been Ludwig slipping into the closet."

Beatrice was feeling annoyed and worried, mostly worried. "Do you think Wolf has our rooms bugged?"

"They probably don't have that kind of technology here," Ollie said, "unless they're using magic."

"That's something we don't know," Beatrice said suddenly. "He thinks that *we're* powerful, but just how powerful is he?"

"*I* think,"Miranda said slowly, "that Wolf didn't ask us to stay here so that he could protect us. He wanted us here so he could keep an eye on us."

Beatrice was afraid that Miranda was right.

9

Too Many Suspects

Beatrice woke up early the next morning to numbing cold. Even though she had the blanket pulled up over her nose, her teeth were chattering and her body felt frozen. Her feet, however, were warm where Cayenne was snuggled up against them under the covers.

Beatrice jumped out of bed and pulled on her clothes, including a sweater her mother had insisted she bring. She brushed her teeth using the icy water in the pitcher, and was just combing her hair when she heard a noise from the street. Jerking on her jacket, Beatrice went over to the window to investigate.

A big, burly man in dark blue robes was knocking on Wolf's door. Cayenne had crawled out of bed, stretching, and now she leaped to the windowsill to see what was going on.

The man's gray hair was clipped short and he appeared reasonably clean, which led Beatrice to whisper to Cayenne, "He doesn't look like a thief. Why don't we go see if we can find out who he is?"

Teddy and Miranda were still asleep, only the tops of their heads showing above the gray blankets. Beatrice left the room quietly, with Cayenne darting after her, and paused to listen at Ollie and Cyrus's door. When she didn't hear anything from inside, she headed for the stairs.

The downstairs hall was empty. Beatrice walked quickly to Wolf's study and sat down on one of the benches beside the closed doors. She could hear voices and realized that one of the doors was standing open about an inch. Beatrice edged over to the door—her need for information outweighing her sense of shame—and listened.

"But I'm responsible for everything that happens here," a man was saying, sounding anxious. "If they ever begin to ask questions at the Witches' Institute, who do you think they'll start with? Tom Duckham, Sheriff of Heraldstone, that's who!"

"Tom, you don't have anything to worry about." This was Wolf speaking, calm and reassuring.

"But with that Beatrice Bailiwick and her crowd here, the Institute's going to be watching," the sheriff insisted. "And if anything happens to one of those kids, investigators will come in and start digging around. It won't take them long to find out that I haven't been doing my job!"

"It's a little late to think about that now," Wolf said, beginning to sound bored. "Anyway, the Institute can't hold you responsible for murders committed by Dally Rumpe."

"So you think he might actually kill them?" the sheriff asked quickly.

"The odds are good, I'd say," Wolf answered, as casually as if he had been making a prediction about the weather. "I don't know how they've managed to beat him so far, but their luck can't hold out forever, can it?"

By this time, Beatrice was fuming. *He could care less if Dally Rumpe kills us*, she thought. *Boy, does Lovie have this guy all wrong. A real gentleman . . . a good heart. Right!*

Cayenne had jumped up on the bench beside Beatrice. Sensing her mistress's distress, the cat placed her front paws in Beatrice's lap and looked up at her with concern in her green-gold eyes. Beatrice stroked the cat absently, thinking that they really needed to get out of this house.

"Perhaps this will ease your worry," Wolf was saying.

Beatrice couldn't see what was happening, so she lifted Cayenne from her lap and stood up, leaning closer to the crack in the door. Wolf was handing a small leather pouch to the sheriff, who didn't hesitate to snatch it away from him.

"Haven't I taken care of you all these years?" Wolf asked, his expression faintly mocking. "Answer me, Tom. Haven't you been well paid to ignore the occasional—indiscretion?"

"Occasional?" Tom Duckham was frowning as he stuffed the pouch inside his robes. "I've had to turn a blind eye to your activities almost every day."

"Just see that you keep doing that," Wolf said briskly, "and everything will be fine. For both of us."

When the sheriff turned to leave, Beatrice scooped up Cayenne and ran to the closet under the stairs. She was standing inside among the mops and brooms, scarcely breathing, when Tom Duckham walked past.

Beatrice waited until she heard the front door close, and was just about to peek out when she heard someone clumping down the hall. That had to be Ludwig, heading for Wolf's study. When the footsteps had faded away, Beatrice opened the door slowly and looked out. One of the doors to the study stood half open.

Beatrice was afraid she'd be caught if she tried to eavesdrop again, but she had to learn as much as she could about Wolf and what he was up to. So she eased out of the closet, still holding Cayenne in her arms, and tiptoed to the door.

Wolf was sitting in a chair in front of the fire with his back to Beatrice. Ludwig was standing nearby, also looking in the direction of the fire.

"—has done all he can," Ludwig was saying in the familiar grumbling voice. "He says John Chew isn't to ride again for a month, and he's to stay here, in bed, for at least a week."

"All right," Wolf said. "Is there anything else?"

"One thing," Ludwig said. "I overheard those obnoxious brats you invited here talking about you last night. They know you're spying on them."

Wolf laughed, but the sound was hollow and cold. "Of course they do—because I *want* them to know! They need to understand who's in charge. You just keep your ears open and report back to me on their plans."

Beatrice watched as Wolf dug a gold coin from a pocket in his robes and handed it to Ludwig. So that was what Ludwig meant about the benefits of working here. But Wolf was really too much. He was paying off *everybody!*

"When did Doc Llewellyn say he'd come by again?" Wolf asked.

"In the morning. He can't come sooner because he has to go to the castle after lunch—and he said he probably wouldn't get back until late."

Beatrice froze. *The castle? Doc Llewellyn was allowed to enter the castle? And Wolf didn't seem the least bit surprised!* But that could only mean . . . What, exactly, *did* it mean? That the doctor was Dally Rumpe? Or Wolf was, and Doc Llewellyn was working for him?

Ludwig seemed ready to leave, so Beatrice hurried down the hall to the stairs. She was halfway up to the second floor when the spriggan passed below her without noticing that she was there.

Beatrice knocked lightly on Ollie and Cyrus's door, and Ollie answered, fully dressed.

"Come over to our room," Beatrice whispered. "I have a lot to tell you."

Teddy and Miranda were also awake and dressed, but Teddy was moaning that she had been cold all night and Miranda was complaining about not being able to take a shower. Then they saw the anxious look on Beatrice's face, and Miranda said, "Spill it, Beatrice. What have you found out?"

When Ollie and Cyrus walked in, Beatrice closed the door and proceeded to tell them everything she had heard.

"So is Wolf paying the sheriff to ignore his men's stealing," Miranda asked, "or is there another reason?"

"I'm not sure," Beatrice replied. "At first, I thought it was for the stealing—but Wolf *could* be paying off Sheriff Duckham because he knows that Wolf is Dally Rumpe."

"Well, those remarks about Dally Rumpe killing us were pretty heartless," Teddy said hotly. "I wouldn't put *anything* past the man."

"He's definitely spying on us," Beatrice said. "Or paying Ludwig and others to do it."

"Maybe Ganef," Ollie said. "Or Blacksheep Jones! I hadn't thought of him before. Blacksheep made such a big deal about not working for Wolf—but he might have just wanted to throw us off."

"Anyway," Beatrice said, "I haven't told you the most important thing yet. Ludwig told Wolf that Doc Llewellyn wouldn't be able to come back and check on John Chew until tomorrow morning—because he's going to the castle this afternoon!"

Everyone just stared at her, dumbfounded.

Finally, Ollie said, "Then the doctor has to be involved somehow with Dally Rumpe!"

"Exactly," Beatrice said darkly. "And whatever that involvement is, Wolf knows all about it."

Beatrice and her companions had lunch at The Galloping Ghost. The day's menu featured stinkbug stew and black bread. Even Ollie, who would eat just about anything, lost his appetite when the stew's odor reached his nose.

"We're going to starve to death," Cyrus said mournfully.

"Just fill up on the bread," Teddy said. She bit into a hunk of the hard black bread and her teeth didn't even make a mark on it.

"There's Doc Llewellyn," Beatrice murmured. "He's just being served. If we leave now, we'll have a good head start."

The others nodded and got up from the table. They had decided to hide near Bailiwick Castle where they could see for themselves if the doctor was really allowed to enter.

When they reached the town gates, Beatrice noticed two men on foot coming through a door in the wall. "Let's try that," she said.

They passed through the door, without anyone seeming to notice them, and started down the road toward the castle.

"Maybe we should stay off the road," Ollie said as they crested the first hill, "in case Doc Llewellyn catches up with us."

"Good idea," Miranda said.

Walking through the tall grass wasn't as easy. But they had managed to reach the top of the second hill, with Bailiwick Castle in full view, when they heard faint hoofbeats on the road behind them.

"Over there!" Teddy exclaimed, pointing at some low bushes just ahead.

They ran to the shrubbery and ducked down behind it. Peering through the foliage, Beatrice could see the road, and in the distance, one side of the castle wall.

A couple of minutes later, they saw a chestnut horse galloping down the road toward them, its pounding hooves kicking up clouds of dust. When the horse drew a little closer, Beatrice could identify the rider. It was Doc Llewellyn.

The horse sped past. Beatrice and her friends raised their heads a little to follow it with their eyes.

"Do we dare go after him?" Teddy asked.

"The goblins might spot us," Ollie said. "Besides, we can see from here if the doc goes inside."

They watched silently as Doc Llewellyn turned onto the road that led to the castle. Beatrice could see the goblins' heads above the wall—dozens of them, maybe even *hundreds*—but no alarm sounded and no flaming arrows came flying through the air. The doctor just rode up to the bridge, and then onto it, crossing the moat to the gates.

"The bridge isn't shaking," Cyrus remarked.

"Look!" Miranda said abruptly. "The gates are opening."

Not only that, but several figures in dark tunics and trousers—goblin guards, Beatrice assumed, although they were too far away for her to see their faces—had come out from the castle yard. One held the reins of the doctor's horse while he dismounted, and the others seemed to be conversing with him. Then the guards and the doctor started walking toward the castle. They entered the yard, and the gates closed behind them.

Beatrice sat back in the grass and blew her bangs out of her eyes.

"The goblins were obviously expecting him," she said. "But wouldn't they have made a bigger fuss over him if he were Dally Rumpe?"

"A lot's missed when you can't hear what's being said," Ollie pointed out. "I don't think we should draw any conclusions just yet."

"Well, there's *one* conclusion we can draw," Miranda said. "Doc Llewellyn was welcomed warmly into Dally Rumpe's stronghold."

"It's certainly suspicious," Beatrice agreed, "but then so are Wolf and Ludwig and Hobnob and Blacksheep Jones . . ."

"And what about John Chew?" Teddy said suddenly. "We don't know anything about him yet."

"And we don't know much about Ganef or Badger," Cyrus said. "Or Pinchgutt. *He* seems nasty enough to be an evil sorcerer."

"Well, we know that Dally Rumpe can take on any appearance he chooses," Ollie said.

"Right," Beatrice replied. "He could be anyone. Even Sheriff Duckham. Or Lovie Fitzsimmons, for that matter."

"I don't know about Lovie," Miranda said. "I don't trust anyone, and even *I* don't get suspicious vibes from Lovie."

"My point exactly," Beatrice said dryly. "Dally Rumpe has managed to fool us four times with his disguises. It's always someone you'd never suspect."

Miranda looked uncertain now.

"There are just too many suspects," Teddy muttered.

10

Spies and Powders

The girls were getting ready for lunch when they heard loud voices. It sounded like men were having an argument right outside their room.

"Is that Wolf?" Teddy asked.

"I think so," Beatrice said, and opened the door to check.

Ollie and Cyrus had come out of their room and were looking down the hall. Wolf was standing in the doorway of the room at the head of the stairs, shouting, "If you try to get out of that bed, I'll tie you down! And you know I mean it."

"I'd like to see you try," came another man's angry voice from inside the room. "While I'm lying here doing nothing, that fancy-pants Blacksheep Jones will be holding up all my coaches—and telling everybody that he's the best!"

"Blacksheep's finest days are behind him," Wolf snapped. "He's getting to be an old man."

"You wouldn't know it, the way he struts around!"

Wolf looked up and saw Beatrice, her friends, and her cat staring at him. He made an impatient gesture with his hand, and said curtly, "Since you seem so interested in a private conversation, come over here and I'll introduce you to the greatest highwayman in the Sphere."

Beatrice and the others obeyed meekly. When they reached the doorway where Wolf was standing, they looked inside and saw John Chew lying in bed against a stack of pillows. Beatrice noticed that the bed was about four times as wide as the cots she and her friends were sleeping on, and was draped with luxurious blue and gold silk hangings.

Wolf ushered them into the room and made the introductions. The highwayman was smiling, appearing pleased to meet them, only the ashen hue of his face betraying the fact that he wasn't a well man.

"I'm glad you're getting better," Beatrice said. "It's probably because of us that you were attacked."

John Chew shook his blond head as if to dismiss her words. "The only one responsible for that attack is Dally Rumpe," he said firmly. "And I, for one, am happy you're here to take care of him!"

"My feelings exactly," Wolf murmured.

The highwayman frowned at Wolf. "You can leave us now," he said. "I'm sure you have some illegal activities to plan. These young people can keep me company for a while."

Wolf looked surprised, and not altogether pleased by the dismissal, but he nodded and said pleasantly enough, "Just don't tire yourself out, John. I've been given orders by Doc Llewellyn to see that you get plenty of rest."

"The old witch doctor," John Chew muttered. Then, when Wolf had left, he added cheerfully, "Will one of you shut that door? Wolf likes knowing everything that's going on, but what I talk about with my visitors is none of his business."

Grinning, Ollie closed the door.

John Chew shifted his position against the pillows and grimaced in pain.

"Can we get you anything?" Beatrice asked quickly.

"No, no, I'm fine," the man said. "That old ghoul Hobnob has been bringing me trays every ten minutes. Probably just keeping an eye on me for Wolf."

Beatrice knew the feeling, but she wondered if Wolf really spied on his own men. "I'm sure they just want you to be comfortable," she replied, and then waited to see what the highwayman would say.

John Chew grinned at her. "You're quite the diplomat, Beatrice Bailiwick, and yes, Wolf Duvall takes good care of his men—but he's not above checking up on us. A man in his position can't be too careful, you know, and Wolf doesn't really trust anyone. That's how he's stayed alive and in control for so long."

Beatrice heard admiration in the man's voice, but she thought it was given grudgingly. Something told her that John Chew would like nothing better than to have Wolf out of the picture, allowing *him* to be in charge.

"So tell me," the highwayman said, "how are you planning to enter the castle?"

"We don't know," Beatrice admitted.

"Do you have any ideas?" Miranda asked.

"I *always* have ideas," he said, "but you may not want to hear them. Do you want to know what I really think?"

They all nodded. Cayenne leaped up on the bed and settled down beside John Chew, as if waiting to hear what he had to say.

"I don't believe *anyone* will be able to approach the castle, much less enter it—not the way things are now. These wounds," he added, placing a hand on his bandaged chest, "prove that Dally Rumpe is determined to keep everyone out—especially you, Beatrice Bailiwick."

"There's one witch who gets in," Cyrus said. "Doc Llewellyn."

John Chew looked interested. "What do you know about the doc?" he asked, staring intently at Cyrus.

Cyrus appeared uncomfortable, like maybe he had said too much. "Nothing, really," he murmured.

"You know *something*," the highwayman said. Then his eyes shifted to Beatrice. "Tell me."

Beatrice didn't see any harm in answering him, so she said, "We saw the doctor ride out to the castle, and the guards let him in as if he were a regular visitor."

A smile tugged at John Chew's mouth. "You were spying on him, were you? Well, good for you. Like Wolf, you can't really afford to trust anyone, can you? Why don't you all sit down, and I'll tell you why Doc Llewellyn is welcomed at the castle."

Miranda and Teddy took the only chairs, and the others perched on the edge of the bed.

"You see," John Chew said, "Doc is the only physician around here, so Dally Rumpe insists that he come to the castle when anyone gets sick. The doc is handsomely paid, of course, but he's terrified every time he has to go out there. He just figures if he can hold out a little longer, he'll be able to retire in luxury."

The highwayman paused, grinning now. "Did you really think that a weakling like Archibald Llewellyn might be in league with Dally Rumpe? Or might actually *be* Dally Rumpe?" He saw the answer in their sheepish expressions, and he laughed. "I know, you can't eliminate anyone as a suspect, but Doc Llewellyn is scared to death of the sorcerer. The only work he does for Dally Rumpe is to doctor residents of the castle. He's been doing it for years, and everyone in town knows it. It's no secret."

"Is anyone else allowed into the castle?" Beatrice asked.

"No one," John Chew said flatly. "And no one's *tried* to get in for as long as *I* can remember. Now, Wolf would like to," he said, seeming amused by the idea. "I know it eats at him. See, Wolf Duvall used to ride the roads like me and like Blacksheep Jones. I have to admit—although it pains me to say it—that Wolf was one of the best, maybe *the* best, that the Sphere has ever known. Then, years ago, he injured his leg pretty badly, and it was never strong enough for him to ride again. But I know he dreams about the old days—he'd *love* to make one more grand hit—and where better than Bailiwick Castle? Still, he makes out all right," John Chew said, his smile mocking now, "with other people doing all the work. I give him a share of what I bring in—it's worth it to be thought of as one of Wolf's men, to have that protection—but he doesn't get as much from me as he does from the others. And he knows better than to expect it."

Beatrice could tell that John Chew's feelings about Wolf were complicated, even contradictory. He certainly admired Wolf, but along with that admiration, John Chew sounded jealous of him—and determined to maintain his independence from Wolf.

"You'd better leave now," the highwayman said abruptly, sinking back into the pillows, "before Wolf sets that nasty spriggan on you."

Beatrice could see that the man was very tired. She stood up, as did the others, and thanked the highwayman for talking with them.

"It's been my pleasure," he said wearily. "And we'll talk again. Maybe I'll think of some way to help you."

Ollie opened the door and almost fell over Ludwig, who was squatting just outside. The spriggan leaped up, looking furious, and then stomped down the hall.

"Was it something we said?" Miranda murmured.

"I'm sure he has *everything* we said memorized," Teddy muttered. "So he can repeat it, word for word, to Wolf."

The Galloping Ghost was as crowded as usual when Beatrice and her companions arrived. They took the last empty table beside the kitchen door, and ordered six servings of the day's special—boiled bullfrog and black beetle bread—but even Cayenne didn't seem to be looking forward to it.

"Wolf's here," Miranda said, unnecessarily, because the leader of the thieves was seated prominently at a table in the center of the room with Pinchgutt and a half dozen other men. Lovie was fluttering around their table, looking more flushed and animated than usual.

"I think Blacksheep was right about Lovie being interested in Wolf," Teddy said. "Look how she's flirting with him."

"And look how he's flirting back," Ollie added with a grin.

"But Lovie said she wouldn't get involved with a thief."

"And *I* said I'd never eat witch food again," Cyrus retorted. "But here I am choking down the *worst* witch food in the Sphere."

About that time, Doc Llewellyn came into the tavern. He stood by the door, looking around until he spotted Beatrice and her friends, and then made a beeline for them.

"Won't you join us?" Ollie asked when the doctor reached their table.

"I can't stay," Doc Llewellyn said, his expression seeming even more severe than normal. "I just wanted to clear something up. I understand that you've been following me."

Ludwig overheard us talking to John Chew and told Wolf, Beatrice thought. *Or had John Chew told the doctor himself?*

"Well, you should know," Doc Llewellyn went on, his voice shaking with indignation, "that I only go to the castle because Dally Rumpe orders me to! I've never even seen him, but all those awful goblins are there, and sometimes I have to treat *them!* And let me tell you, that isn't a pleasant task."

"What about Bromwich?" Beatrice asked quickly. "Have you ever seen him?"

Doc Llewellyn looked startled by the question. Then his face closed up and his eyes slid away from hers.

"You *have* seen him," Miranda said triumphantly.

"I'm—not supposed to talk about what happens inside the castle," the doctor said uneasily, "but, yes, I have treated Bromwich a few times. Dally Rumpe sees that he receives medical care—probably because he enjoys keeping his brother a prisoner so much, he doesn't want to lose him."

"Bromwich is in a dungeon under the castle, isn't he?" Ollie asked.

Doc Llewellyn nodded curtly. "But don't ask me how to get there—I couldn't tell you, even if I wanted to. The goblins always blindfold me. But I do know that the corridors are a maze. You'd never find your way to the dungeon." Then he stopped, a look of dread on his face. "And there's a horrible creature named Zortag, who guards Bromwich. I've never seen him, but I've *heard* him—panting and growling, somewhere near Bromwich's cell. It was terrifying!"

Doc Llewellyn was trembling now, and Beatrice thought that he really must be frightened. Either that, or he was an exceptional actor.

"Don't ask me anything else," the physician said, backing away from the table. "And if you know what's good for you, you'll stay far away from that castle!"

He spun around and scurried for the door, just as Folly arrived with their meals. The ghost hovered several feet above them, dropping each plate so that it clattered and bounced as it hit the table. Miranda's landed too close to the edge and slid upside down into her lap. She let out a screech and then glared up at the phantom, who was chuckling merrily. His amusement at her expense was too much for Miranda. She started to scream insults at him, which only added to Folly's enjoyment of the moment. He was shrieking with laughter as he zoomed back toward the kitchen.

"That awful, horrible—" Miranda struggled to find the right word, and finally settled for "*ghost!* Lovie should have him exorcized. Or whatever they do to ghosts."

She went on muttering as she scraped gummy gray globs—boiled bullfrogs, presumably—off her lap and back onto the plate.

"Let me help you," Beatrice said, and began mopping up bullfrog juice from her cousin's arm.

"Miranda, I'll be glad to share *my* lunch with you," Cyrus said with complete sincerity.

"We'll *all* be happy to share our lunches," Ollie added.

By this time, Miranda had calmed down a little. She began to giggle. "I guess I should look at the bright side," she said. "At least I won't have to *eat* this now."

They ate their black beetle bread, which was alarmingly crunchy, but at least soft enough to chew, and were getting ready to leave when Ganef approached the table.

"So how's everything going?" Ganef asked. "Have you found a way into the castle?"

"We're still working on it," Beatrice answered evasively.

"Well," Ganef said, lowering his voice so that no one beyond the table could hear, "maybe I can help."

He reached inside his tunic and withdrew something, while glancing around to see if anyone was watching. His fingers were curved around the object, so Beatrice couldn't see what it was until he slipped it into her hand. It was a small glass vial containing a finely ground powder that looked like cinnamon. There was a label on the glass. Beatrice leaned closer and read: *Invisibility Powders*, followed by directions for how to use them.

Beatrice's head jerked up. "Does this stuff really work?" she asked Ganef.

He shrugged. "I haven't tried it. But it says that you can sprinkle the powders on yourself and be completely invisible for an hour."

"Where did you get this?" Ollie asked, reaching for the vial to study it.

"Don't let anybody see it," Ganef said quickly. "I should've turned it over to Wolf, but I forgot about having it. I took it off a guy who was traveling through Heraldstone awhile back. A witch scholar named Most Worthy Piddle."

Everyone's face showed instant recognition of the name.

"We know him," Beatrice said to Ganef. "We met him on our first trip to the Sphere."

"Well, everybody says he's really powerful," Ganef said, "so I figure the powders must work. I was disappointed at first—what I was after was gold or silver. Then

I thought being invisible might be helpful in my line of work. But I think you need the powders more than I do."

"Thank you, Ganef," Beatrice said. She was touched by his generosity—but there was still that niggling worry: Could they trust him?

After Ganef had left, Beatrice slipped the vial into the pocket of her jacket. "Well, what do you think?" she asked. "Should we try it?"

Teddy was frowning. "You don't suppose Wolf—or someone else—put Ganef up to this, do you? What if these aren't invisibility powders at all? What if they turn us into—*ferrets* or something?"

"Or what if someone just wants to make sure that we *do* get inside the castle?" Miranda asked. "And once we're there, they'll give us a cell next to Bromwich."

"I *think* we can trust Ganef," Ollie said, but he didn't appear totally convinced.

"I guess we have to try it," Beatrice concluded. "And the sooner the better. I vote that we leave for the castle tonight."

"So do I," Teddy said, still frowning.

The others nodded their agreement.

"Let's go for a walk around town," Beatrice said, "and make plans. I don't want to discuss anything important in Wolf's house."

She glanced over at Wolf's table and was unnerved when she met his eyes. He was watching them, smiling faintly. Beatrice had the disturbing feeling that he knew a lot more than they did.

11

On the Shaking Bridge

Beatrice and her companions waited in their rooms until dark. Then they crept down the stairs, and seeing no one, left Wolf's house.

Once out on the street, Ollie whispered to Beatrice, "Did you bring the invisibility powders?"

"They're in my pocket."

"Let's get away from here," Cyrus said nervously, "before anyone sees us."

They headed down the street in the direction of the town gates, with Cayenne running slightly ahead. A three-quarter moon was rising, and once high in the sky, would provide them with light. But for the moment, they had to depend on the few lanterns lit on street corners and the candlelight from windows of surrounding houses. Actually, Beatrice was comforted by the darkness, thinking that no one would notice them leaving town. But then she glanced back at Wolf's house—and what she saw stopped her in her tracks.

"What is it?" Miranda asked sharply.

"There's someone on Wolf's doorstep," Beatrice replied. "I think it's Hobnob."

They all looked back and saw an enormous figure standing in front of Wolf's door. It had to be Hobnob because no one else in town was quite that broad.

"He's going back inside," Cyrus said.

"No doubt, to tell Wolf that we're leaving," Ollie added.

"If Wolf is Dally Rumpe," Beatrice said, "or even working for him, we're in trouble."

"All the more reason to get out of here," Teddy declared, and took off down the street.

The others followed, moving so quickly they were all a little breathless when they finally reached the main gates.

"Come here, Cayenne," Beatrice called out softly.

The cat padded over to Beatrice and leaped into the girl's outstretched arms.

No one else was near the gates, and the door was still unlocked. Beatrice and her companions passed through silently and started down the road toward Bailiwick Castle.

The moon was high enough now to cast a silver sheen over the road and the hills. They made good time, and were just starting up the second hill when they heard hoofbeats on the road ahead. Without hesitating, they jumped into a ditch alongside the road and hid in the tall grass.

Soon a horse and rider crested the hill and came galloping down the sloping road toward them. The moonlight was bright enough for Beatrice to make out the horseman's pale robes and skinny frame. It was definitely Doc Llewellyn!

The horse and rider passed them swiftly, and as they disappeared down the road, Beatrice said, "The doc seems to spend an awful lot of time at the castle. Can that many goblins be sick?"

"It is suspicious," Ollie agreed. "Maybe he's just pretending to see patients as a cover for something else."

"John Chew believes him," Teddy said.

"And who's to say John Chew is telling the truth?" Miranda demanded. "There's something about that highwayman that makes me uneasy."

"The only thing I've picked up from John Chew," Ollie said, "is that he's ambitious."

"So is Dally Rumpe," Miranda shot back.

"So are you," Teddy pointed out mildly.

"Like you're *not*," Miranda snapped. "All I'm saying is there seem to be a number of people who fit the Dally Rumpe profile—arrogant, self-absorbed, and driven by ambition. Besides you and me, Teddy," Miranda added drily. "John Chew is one of them, and Wolf's another. And John Chew told us that Doc Llewellyn is trying to amass a fortune so he can retire and leave Heraldstone for good. That sounds pretty ambitious to me."

"We aren't going to figure anything out sitting in this ditch," Beatrice said. "I think we'd better get moving."

Staying off the road, they walked as close as they dared to the castle before squatting down in the tall grass to talk over how to proceed. Torches blazed all around the top of the castle wall, and in their glow, Beatrice and her companions could see guards posted every few feet.

"The invisibility powders only last an hour," Beatrice said, "so we shouldn't use them until the last minute."

"Yeah," Miranda agreed. "Once we're in the castle, who knows how long it will take to find Bromwich."

"I think Cyrus should shrink us now," Ollie said. "That way, we'll be able to move closer before we use the powders."

"Okay," Teddy said, "let's do it."

Beatrice picked up Cayenne, and the five witches reached out to take one another's hands. Then Cyrus began to chant:

> By the mysteries, one and all,
> Make us shrink from tall to small.
> Cut us down to inches three,
> As my will, so mote it be.

Beatrice had never gotten used to the feeling of being sucked down a drain, swirling around and around and around until she was too dizzy to stand. But when her head finally stopped spinning, she saw that everyone, including Cayenne, was only three inches tall. The grass in which they were sitting was at least ten times taller than they were.

"It'll take forever to try to fight our way through the grass," Ollie said. "I don't think the goblins will see us if we walk along the edge of the road until we reach the turnoff to the castle."

They struggled through the grass to the road, and staying as close as possible to the edge, started for the castle.

Twenty minutes later, they reached the spot where a narrower road branched off to take them to the castle gates.

"We can't go any farther without being seen," Teddy said, sounding a little anxious.

"Beatrice, I guess it's time to try the powders," Ollie said.

Beatrice reached into her jacket pocket and withdrew the vial, which had also been shrunk.

"Did you read the directions?" Cyrus asked.

"The label said to take a small pinch and sprinkle it over the head of the person you want to make invisible," Beatrice said. She pulled the cork from the vial and poured a tiny bit of the powders into her palm. "Okay, here goes," she said, her heart beginning to thump against her ribs. "Who wants to go first?"

"I will," Miranda said.

Beatrice picked up a small amount of the brown powder with the tips of her thumb and index finger and sprinkled it over Miranda's head.

Miranda's shoulders twitched and she giggled softly. "It tickles," she said.

And then she disappeared. Just like that!

"It works!" Teddy exclaimed, the delight in her voice mixed with awe. "Miranda, where are you?"

"Standing right beside you," came Miranda's disembodied voice. "So you really can't see me?"

"Nope," Cyrus said cheerfully. "I'll go next, Beatrice."

Beatrice sprinkled the powders over each of them, finishing up with Cayenne and then herself, and one by one, their images disappeared.

"This is so cool," Teddy said. "We'll be able to breeze right into the castle."

"Let's not get too confident," Beatrice cautioned. "Even as light as we are, the bridge may still be able to sense us. And for all I know, goblins might have the power to see us even if we're invisible to each other."

"Well, there's only one way to find out," Ollie said.

"Maybe we should hold hands so we'll be sure to stay together," Beatrice said, "and Cayenne can ride on my shoulder."

She felt a hand fumble for hers and clasp it. "Ollie?"

"It's me," Ollie answered. "All right, let's go."

The invisible party started down the road toward the castle. Beatrice felt a knot of fear in her stomach as they walked steadily toward the bridge. She knew that Ollie must be frightened, too, because his grip on her hand had tightened until it was almost painful. And Cayenne's claws were digging into her shoulder.

When they reached the edge of the moat, they stopped. On the other side of the dark water were enormous double gates set into the castle wall. A two-inch crack beneath the gates gave them plenty of room to slip into the castle yard. Amazingly, there was only silence all around them. *If the goblins could see us*, Beatrice thought, *they would have sounded the alarm and started attacking us by now.* But all was peaceful and still within the castle walls.

"Everybody ready?" Ollie whispered. "Let's step on the bridge together, on the count of three. One. Two. Three."

The five stepped forward, their feet touching the bridge at the same moment. Instantly, the wooden bridge began to shudder and buck. And howl! As Beatrice was thrown down onto the rough planks, a deafening sound that was half screech and half moan rose up around her. She would have covered her ears, but she had bounced to the very edge of the bridge—was actually looking down into the dark, swirling water below—and she needed both hands to cling to the end of the plank. Then she saw something moving in the water, glistening huge and white in the moonlight. *Fish*, Beatrice realized, *giant, flesh-eating fish*. There were dozens of them—some at least ten feet long!

Still hanging onto the writhing, jerking plank, Beatrice looked around in panic for her companions—and then remembered that they were invisible! For all she knew, they could have been tossed into the water with those hungry fish!

It was hard to think with the bridge bucking like a bronco beneath her, but Beatrice knew that the only way to save herself was to somehow manage to get off the bridge and back to land. But if she let go of the plank, she would almost certainly be flung into the water. Her fingers were already beginning to cramp, and her arms were aching from exertion. Beatrice knew she wouldn't be able to hang on much longer—and she decided to act. Without pausing to consider the risks, she pulled her knees up until her feet were flat on the bridge, released her grip on the plank, and literally threw herself toward solid ground.

She landed on a hard surface, one that was blessedly still. Then she realized that her face was pressed into the dirt. She'd made it! Sitting up, Beatrice saw that the bridge was so close she could have touched it with her foot, but she was in the middle of the road, safe.

As the thought of safety filled her with dizzying relief, Beatrice saw the balls of flame shooting by all around her—and she realized that they were flaming arrows. The goblins on the castle wall were aiming wildly, and the night sky was filled with arrows—whizzing from the goblins' bows like glowing comets, lighting up the sky until it looked as if the sun were rising over the bridge.

Suddenly Beatrice became aware of an intense stabbing in her shoulder. Cayenne! She reached up and felt the cat's bristling fur. Miraculously, Cayenne had held on. Beatrice grabbed for the cat, and holding her protectively, began to call out names. *"Ollie! Teddy! Cyrus! Miranda!"*

There were answering calls, sounding faint and strangled, but with fiery arrows still falling around her and the howling of the bridge, Beatrice couldn't identify the voices or tell where they were coming from. She could only hope that everyone had made it back to solid ground.

Suddenly an arrow struck the earth only inches away from where Beatrice sat. Leaping to her feet, she screamed, "Run!" And with Cayenne clutched to her chest, Beatrice raced for the main road as fast as her diminutive stature would allow.

Beatrice made it to the road and into the grass beyond before she collapsed, gasping for air. She turned back to the castle and saw that the sky was still filled with shooting flames, but the bridge was no longer bucking or howling. Then Beatrice saw the grass at the edge of the road begin to part and bend, as if someone were walking through it.

"I'm here!" Beatrice called out.

"Beatrice?" It was Ollie's voice coming toward her. Then Teddy's. Then Cyrus's. Beatrice felt them brush against her as they fell to the ground. But where was Miranda?

"*Miranda!*" Beatrice screamed. Over and over she called, her short-lived relief quickly turning to fear. Had Miranda not made it off the bridge? Or had one of the arrows hit her?

But then Beatrice saw the grass part once again, and she heard a breathless voice. It wasn't until Miranda collapsed nearby that Beatrice could make out what she was saying.

"This was . . . the most idiotic plan . . . you amateurs . . . have come up with . . . yet," Miranda said between pants.

"Oh, and I suppose you have a better idea?" Teddy's voice sounded weak and irritated.

"*Light-years* better," came Miranda's blunt response.

"So tell us," Beatrice said.

"Wolf offered to help us," Miranda said, still trying to control her breathing. "I say we should take him up on it."

"But what if he can't be trusted?" Cyrus asked, sounding worried. "What if—"

"*Nothing*," Miranda cut in brusquely, "could turn out any worse than this!"

12

The Hidden Passage

When Beatrice and her companions woke up late the next morning, their bodies ached and they felt discouraged. The house was almost eerily quiet as they left for breakfast. John Chew's door was closed, and there was no sign of Wolf, Hobnob, or Ludwig.

By the time they entered The Galloping Ghost, most of the breakfast crowd had left, and Beatrice's group had its choice of tables. The only diners they knew were Pinchgutt, who was sitting with two other men, and Blacksheep Jones, seated at a table by himself.

Lovie came bustling over to Beatrice's table, wearing her heartiest smile. But when she noticed Folly hovering in the air behind her with an especially malicious grin, Lovie glared at the ghost and said crossly, "Go on back to the kitchen, you foul, despicable troublemaker, you. *I'll* serve the Bailiwick party, thank you."

Folly just chortled wildly and began to jet around the room, making occasional nosedives into diners' plates. Lovie watched him, scowling.

"He's already stuck a fork in poor Woozy Bloom's ear," Lovie fumed to Beatrice and her friends, "and Blacksheep Jones is ready to strangle him."

Beatrice thought about asking what Folly had done to Blacksheep, but after two days of barely edible food, she was starving. Still, she had to brace herself to ask, "What's on the menu this morning?"

"Wash-brew, sow-bug bread, and wood-tick tea."

Beatrice decided there was no point in asking Lovie to describe the dishes—she probably didn't want to know, anyway—and said, "That's what I'll have then."

The others nodded, their faces resigned.

After they were served, Beatrice found out that the wood-tick tea was just as wretched as it sounded, but the sow-bug bread wasn't too terrible if she didn't focus on the whole insects scattered throughout. And the wash-brew was something very much like oatmeal sweetened with honey. Everyone at the table scarfed down the wash-brew and requested second helpings. Cayenne wasn't a fan of oatmeal, but the dragon's milk poured over it was very much to her liking.

They were just finishing up, and feeling better than they had in days, when Blacksheep Jones stopped by their table on his way out. He was as immaculate and grand as ever in crimson silk and black velvet, but Beatrice was shocked to see that one eye was swollen shut and beginning to turn purple, and there was a prominent lump on his forehead.

"What happened to you?" Miranda burst out before the highwayman had even greeted them.

Blacksheep Jones's one good eye narrowed to an angry slit. "That maniac of a ghost swung an iron kettle at me." He spoke quietly, but there was no mistaking the fury in his voice. "I'm going to hire a ghost trapper *today* and get that wispy little weasel out of here once and for all."

"Maybe you ought to see Doc Llewellyn," Ollie said. "That bump on your head could be serious."

The highwayman waved an impatient hand. "It would take more than that little squirt can dish out to do me in. But I didn't come over here to talk about my health," he added briskly, looking now at Beatrice. "I heard about your bad luck last night—not being able to enter the castle. By the way, where in the world did you get invisibility powders?"

Beatrice's mouth fell open. "How did *you* know we went to the castle?"

Blacksheep smiled, apparently enjoying being one who was in the know. "Word gets around in Heraldstone," he replied vaguely. "Anyway, I just wanted to express my regrets. I'm sure you'll do better next time."

The highwayman bowed gallantly, plumed hat to his chest, and left before anyone at the table had fully recovered.

"How did he *know*?" Teddy muttered.

"Hobnob saw us leave and told Wolf," Cyrus said.

"And Wolf told Blacksheep?" Ollie asked, looking puzzled. "I don't think they even talk to each other."

"Oh, what difference does it make?" Miranda asked impatiently. "The point is, everyone in town knows everything we're doing. We'd better keep that in mind in the future."

"And you still think we should ask for Wolf's help?" Teddy asked, cutting her eyes at Miranda. "You trust him enough to follow his advice?"

Miranda gave Teddy a cool look. "Unless you have a better idea, O Brilliant One."

"All we need now is to fight with each other," Beatrice cut in, frowning.

She was about to say more when she noticed Ganef and Badger coming through the front door. Ganef saw Beatrice and waved. Then the two boys made straight for her table.

"Beatrice," Ganef said, "I'm really sorry the invisibility powders didn't work."

Beatrice's eyebrows shot up.

"How did you hear about our trip to the castle?" Ollie asked.

"Pinchgutt told me," Ganef said promptly, with no apparent guile.

"And who told Pinchgutt?" Beatrice asked.

Ganef shook his head. "I don't know. Some thief or other. Anyhow, *everybody* knows about it now. I just wish it had turned out better."

The boy sounded sincere, and Beatrice smiled at him. "Actually, the invisibility powders worked perfectly," she assured him. "It was the shaking bridge that didn't cooperate. But we used all the powders, I'm afraid."

"That's all right," Ganef said. "I wanted you to have them, and they wouldn't have done me much good, anyway. I haven't found a pocket to pick in two days."

"Three days for me," Badger added woefully. "Even my explosions don't help anymore. Sure, they distract people, but I can dip into a dozen pockets, and if I come up with a ragged hanky, I'm lucky."

Ganef was studying Beatrice's face, frowning under the weight of his thoughts. "It's Wolf you need to go to," Ganef said. "He knows things that might help you."

"What sorts of things?" Beatrice asked.

The boy shrugged, looking uneasy. "We've gotta be going," he said. "Just talk to Wolf."

"See?" Miranda said when the boys were gone, sounding a little smug. "I told you we need to ask for Wolf's help. That little pickpocket knows something."

There was still no one around when Beatrice and her companions went back to Wolf's house. But they were just passing John Chew's room when the door opened and Doc Llewellyn stepped out into the hall. He appeared startled to see them and closed the door quickly behind him.

"How's your patient this morning?" Beatrice asked.

"Better," the physician said curtly, but his face was as somber as ever.

"We saw you coming back from Bailiwick Castle last night," Beatrice went on, watching for a reaction.

And she got one. The doctor's pasty face seemed to turn paler still, and one eye began to twitch.

"There . . . there was . . . an illness at the castle," he muttered, stumbling over the words, "although I don't see that I owe you an explanation."

With that, Doc Llewellyn pushed past them and hurried down the stairs.

"He sure gets nervous when we mention the castle," Teddy remarked.

"Guilty conscience?" Miranda suggested.

"Or maybe having to go there is just getting to him," Ollie said.

"If only we could have heard what the guards said to him," Beatrice murmured, then stopped abruptly. "Do you hear that?"

They stood very still, listening, and sure enough, there was the muffled sound of someone talking. Beatrice took a step toward the wall opposite John Chew's door.

"It's coming from here," she whispered, "but there isn't enough space for a room behind this wall."

"And there's no door," Teddy said softly.

"That we can see," Ollie added.

He walked over to the wall and began to move his hands lightly across the plaster.

"There's a seam here," Ollie said suddenly. "I can feel it running straight up to the ceiling."

"A secret door?" Teddy asked.

"I don't know," Ollie said, pressing on the wall.

Suddenly, a panel about two feet wide swung open into what looked like a small closet.

Teddy gasped. "It *is* a door!"

"Shhh!" Beatrice warned her.

Ollie pushed the panel all the way open, and stepped inside. Then he turned back to them, grinning, and said softly, "There's a staircase in the back corner. I guess it leads down to the first floor."

Cayenne had followed Ollie into the closet, and now she disappeared down the stairs.

"Cayenne!" Beatrice hissed, but the cat didn't reappear.

"I have to go after her," Beatrice said, and hurried into the closet.

As she started down the stairs, Ollie said, "We'll all go," and followed after her.

The staircase was steep and narrow. And completely dark. Something brushed lightly against Beatrice's face, and she jerked back, nearly falling off the narrow step. *Must be cobwebs*, she thought, hoping that was all they would find here.

She could reach out about a foot on either side and feel rough walls. But she couldn't see anything, and the air was stale and musty. She didn't like it. *Not at all!* Then it occurred to her that if someone were to close the upstairs panel, they might be trapped in here forever.

The old wooden steps creaked a little as Beatrice and the others made their way deeper and deeper into the black pit. But now Beatrice realized that there were at least two voices—voices that were becoming more and more distinct as she descended.

Finally, she came to the end of the staircase. Reaching out in the darkness to touch the walls, she could tell that she was in another closet, about the same size as the one upstairs. When Ollie and the others joined her, they were packed tightly into the cramped space, but Beatrice managed to stoop down and feel around until she touched Cayenne's plumed tail.

The voices were quite loud now. They were coming from the other side of the closet wall, and Beatrice realized that they belonged to Wolf and to Doc Llewellyn.

"It has to stop!" the doctor stormed. "Everywhere I go, there they are. Why did you ever ask them to come here?"

"I have my reasons," Wolf replied, his voice cool. "Frankly, Archibald, I'm surprised that you're letting this bunch of ineffectual children get to you this way."

Beatrice bristled, and she heard Miranda mutter, "*Ineffectual*, are we? Well, we'll just see about that!"

Then Beatrice felt Miranda lean against the wall—and suddenly, a panel in the wall swung open. Beatrice, with Cayenne in her arms, Miranda, and Cyrus toppled out of the closet onto a thick Oriental rug. Ollie and Teddy were still standing in the closet with their mouths hanging open.

Beatrice's eyes darted around the room. They were in Wolf's study, and Wolf and Doc Llewellyn were standing about three feet away staring down at the pile of witches on the floor. Doc Llewellyn looked shocked, but Wolf just seemed annoyed.

The doctor turned to Wolf. "You see?" he demanded. "They're always following me!"

Still sitting on the floor, Beatrice said coldly, "We wouldn't *have* to follow you if you weren't always doing something suspicious."

Then Wolf did something totally unexpected. He threw his head back and started to laugh. Doc Llewellyn looked at the thief as if he had lost his mind.

Still laughing, Wolf motioned for the witches at his feet to get up. "And you two," he said to Teddy and Ollie, "come out of there."

"Outrageous," Doc Llewellyn muttered. "Absolutely outrageous."

Wolf's amusement was quickly spent, and he looked around at the young witches with a strange expression on his face. Beatrice couldn't tell if he was angry or perplexed—or *what*. But he was obviously thinking hard about something.

"Go on about your business," Wolf said to the doctor. "You don't need to stay."

"But—"

"I said, *go*," Wolf snapped, and then added, "*I'll* take care of our young friends here."

He had spoken quietly. *Too* quietly. His expression was hard to read, but those sharp eyes seemed to slice through Beatrice's face.

Her heart was pounding, and she found herself wishing again that she had never agreed to stay in this man's house.

But it was too late now.

13

Thieves' Lair

Doc Llewellyn left reluctantly, muttering under his breath. Wolf motioned toward the chairs near the fireplace, and Beatrice and her friends sat down. Beatrice noticed that they all looked as nervous as she felt. Even Cayenne was sitting rigidly on Beatrice's shoulder, ready to make a run for it, if necessary.

Wolf sank into a chair across from them. He studied their faces for an uncomfortably long moment before reaching for a bellpull on the wall and giving it a tug. A moment later, Ludwig stomped into the room.

"Bring my friends some drinks," Wolf told the glowering spriggan. "Dragon's milk for the cat and our own special brew for the others. I'll have my usual."

Ludwig grunted in acknowledgment, spun around, and stomped out of the study.

"What exactly is your 'own special brew'?" Teddy asked warily.

Wolf's smile was less amused than ironic. "Are you concerned that I might try to poison you?" he asked, eyebrows raised in mock dismay. "Have no fear, my young friends. In the first place, you're my guests. What bad manners to poison one's guests. And in the second place, poison isn't the method I would use if I wanted to get rid of you. Too subtle for an old outlaw like me. And in the third place," he said, his smile widening, "I don't wish to do away with you. I still want you to break Dally Rumpe's spell. And you can't very well do that if you're dead, now can you?"

"Do you really believe that five *ineffectual children* can break the spell?" Miranda asked, her gray eyes as icy as her voice.

"That's the single most compelling reason I know not to eavesdrop," Wolf said pleasantly. "You might not like what you hear. But, actually, I only said that to the doc so that he'd worry less. He thinks you're out to get him."

"We are," Beatrice said calmly, "if he turns out to be Dally Rumpe."

Wolf gave a short laugh. "Doc Llewellyn? His magic isn't strong enough to cure a hangnail. I can assure you, Doc is not Dally Rumpe."

Ludwig brought the drinks, and Beatrice noticed Wolf smirking as he watched them move the mugs hesitantly to their lips. Almost defiantly, Beatrice took a big gulp and was amazed to find that it tasted good. *Very* good. The others took a sip and had the same look of surprise on their faces. And since no one was keeling over or frothing at the mouth, Beatrice began to relax a little.

"You can go now, Ludwig," Wolf said to the spriggan, who was still hanging around.

Ludwig made a face that was uglier than his usual one, and then headed for the door, slamming it behind him.

Wolf was watching Beatrice again over the rim of his mug. "You don't have the faintest idea what you're doing, do you?" he asked softly.

Before Beatrice could voice her indignation, Wolf added quickly, "I didn't mean that as an insult, only as a fact. You don't know how to get into the castle now that your shrinking spell and invisibility powders have failed. Am I correct about that?"

"We're working on a new plan," Beatrice said stiffly.

"After hearing of your previous victories over Dally Rumpe," Wolf said, "I had expected your talents to be, shall we say, more sophisticated."

Beatrice looked steadily at him. "We may not be the greatest witches in the Sphere," she said, "but I don't see anyone else trying to break the spell. So if you want Dally Rumpe out of here, I guess we're the only hope you've got."

Wolf blinked, then a smile of genuine amusement spread across his lips. "Good point," he said. "And since you and I have the same goal, I'm going to share some information that may help you."

Beatrice's heart sped up. The others leaned forward, wary, but anxious to hear what he had to say.

"You know that staircase you took when you *dropped in* awhile ago?" Wolf asked. "Well, beneath a trapdoor in that closet is another set of stairs that goes down past the cellar to a series of tunnels."

When he didn't continue, Ollie asked, "Where do the tunnels lead?"

"They spread out in all directions under the town," Wolf said, "and if you take the right one, you'll end up at Bailiwick Castle."

Beatrice heard Teddy's sharp intake of breath and saw Cyrus's eyes grow huge in his small face.

"You mean," Beatrice said, "we could enter the castle from underground. Then why haven't you tried it?"

"That's a fair question," Wolf replied evenly. "I haven't tried it because entering that castle would be dangerous under any circumstances. My great-grandfather, Sam Hill Duvall, was the last to attempt it using the tunnels, and he didn't make it back."

"How do you know one of the tunnels leads to the castle?" Beatrice asked.

Wolf was smiling faintly again. "Because my great-great-great-grandfather, Ebenezer Duvall, used the tunnel all the time to rob Bromwich. According to the story that's been passed down through my family since old Ebenezer's time, he used a concealed entrance to enter Bromwich's Treasure Room. Supposedly, Bromwich was never able to find out how Ebenezer got in."

"But that was more than two hundred years ago," Teddy pointed out. "Dally Rumpe probably found the entrance to the Treasure Room long ago and sealed it up."

"Maybe," Wolf said with a shrug, "and maybe not. But it's worth checking out, isn't it?"

"I think we have to," Miranda murmured.

"But the tunnels run all over the place," Wolf said. "You could get lost forever down there without a map. They were designed that way deliberately, with hidden rooms and lots of dead ends. You see, in Bromwich's time, thieves were tracked by the law and they needed a place to hide out until things cooled down. Ebenezer and his men created this maze of crisscrossing tunnels so that no one would ever be able to find them. They called it Thieves' Lair."

"Do you have a map of the tunnels?" Ollie asked.

Wolf got up and walked over to his desk. He unlocked a drawer and withdrew a rolled-up sheet of parchment.

"The route to the castle is marked in red," Wolf said, handing the map to Beatrice. He sat down facing her again, and added, "But making it to the castle is only the first step. The Treasure Room is bound to be heavily guarded and probably locked from the outside. Even if you manage to reach it through the tunnels, you might not be able to get out into the rest of the castle. Then you'd have to find your way to the dungeon where Bromwich is kept—and I don't have a map of the castle. Then, of course, there's Zortag, the monster that guards Bromwich—and I don't have any idea how you'd get past him. So . . . this map isn't going to solve all your problems."

Beatrice thanked Wolf and stood up, gripping the map in her hand. She didn't know whether to be grateful to the thief or more worried than ever. The main question was, *Could they trust him—or was he leading them into a trap?*

They left Wolf's study and went back upstairs, discussing how they should proceed.

"I have an idea," Beatrice said. "When Pinchgutt warned us about Wolf, he mentioned that he can walk through walls. That might come in handy, if he'd agree to go with us."

"You mean, he could walk through the wall of the Treasure Room," Ollie said, "and then let us out into the castle from the other side."

"If there still *is* a Treasure Room," Miranda said, "and if the tunnels haven't been destroyed."

They were passing John Chew's room, and the door was open. The highwayman called out to them.

"So Wolf gave you the map," he said, his eyes resting on the roll of parchment in Beatrice's hand. "I wondered if he'd tell you about the tunnels."

"Then you know about them," Beatrice said as she approached the bed.

The highwayman nodded. "Not many do, but Wolf's family and mine have been working together for generations, so I know most of the Duvalls' secrets."

"We can't be sure the tunnel to the castle is still open until we go down there," Ollie said. "Or that the entrance to the Treasure Room hasn't been sealed off."

"I heard you mention Pinchgutt," John Chew said. "That's a good idea about taking him along. *If* he'll cooperate. He's not really the helpful type. But if you could convince him that he's pulling one over on Wolf, he might do it. And the idea of having access to the Treasure Room should appeal to him."

Beatrice thought that the highwayman seemed pretty interested in the Treasure Room, himself. His blue eyes gleamed when he mentioned it.

"I'm in no shape to help you right now," John Chew went on, "but if you could wait a few days, I'd be glad to go with you."

I'll bet you would, Beatrice thought.

"Imagine all the loot Bromwich much have stowed away in there," the highwayman mused. "And Dally Rumpe has probably added plenty to it. I wouldn't mind flashing some diamonds and rubies in Blacksheep Jones's face, let me tell you."

"We appreciate the offer," Beatrice said, "but we need to leave as soon as possible."

John Chew's face fell. "Oh, of course. I understand." Then he frowned. "Just don't let anyone know when you're going. Not even Wolf. Or Doc Llewellyn, either."

Beatrice was surprised by this. "Don't you trust Wolf?" she asked. "And the doctor—You said he only goes to the castle because Dally Rumpe orders him to."

"That's right," the highwayman said curtly. "But who knows what either of them would do if they had the chance to cart away a fortune in gold and jewels? Just watch out for yourself, Beatrice Bailiwick. And don't trust anyone."

"Even you?" Teddy asked lightly.

John Chews' intense blue eyes shifted to Teddy's face. "Even me," he said.

14

Into the Maze

Beatrice and her companions spent the rest of the morning wandering through streets and alleys in search of Pinchgutt, with no luck.

Finally, Miranda said, "It's nearly time for lunch. We'll probably find him at The Galloping Ghost."

"Yeah," Ollie said with a grin. "I've never known him to miss a meal."

"No wonder they call him Pinchgutt," Cyrus muttered. "Eating that awful food sure causes a pinch in *my* gut."

The tavern was packed with noontime diners, but there was no sign of Pinchgutt.

"Well, we have to eat," Beatrice said with a noticeable lack of enthusiasm, "so we might as well have lunch and hope he shows up."

The day's offering was some sort of meat pie (Beatrice refused to let Lovie identify what *kind* of meat) and acorn bread soaked in eel oil. The meat was mostly gristle and the bread was rather slippery, but neither tasted as bad as Beatrice had expected. Lovie brought Cayenne a bowl of dragon's milk.

"I never thought I'd see the day when Cay looked thin," Beatrice said, eying the cat as Cayenne lapped up her milk. "This trip has been great for her diet."

"We're all going to be nothing but skin and bones if we have to stay in this town much longer," Teddy muttered.

They were nearly finished with their meal when Pinchgutt finally strode into the tavern. There didn't appear to be any vacant seats, so he walked over to the table where Ganef was sitting and elbowed the young pickpocket in the ribs to make him move down. Ganef slid along the bench, muttering under his breath, until he was crammed up against a protesting Badger. Pinchgutt ignored their complaints and plopped down on the end of the bench.

"We should probably wait till he's alone to talk to him," Ollie said.

"I don't see why," Miranda responded. "If he agrees to go to the castle with us, you know he'll be bragging about it to everyone."

"That's probably true," Teddy agreed. "Besides, it's impossible to keep a secret in Heraldstone. The outlaw grapevine's faster than e-mail."

"Okay," Ollie said, "then let's go talk to him."

Pinchgutt eyed the group warily as they approached his table. Ganef and Badger's expressions were friendly but also blatantly curious.

"Well, look who's here," Pinchgutt said. "I heard about your unfortunate run-in with the shaking bridge. So have you come to tell old Pinchgutt 'so long' before you leave town?"

144

"Oh, we aren't leaving," Beatrice said, sounding a lot sassier than she felt. "We have another plan for entering the castle, and we want you to be part of it."

Pinchgutt's jaw dropped. Then, recovering quickly, the thief said, "You want *me* to be part of it." His lips spread into a sly smile, revealing brown and broken teeth. "Well—Am I the lucky one or what? You know I wouldn't want to pass up a chance to—*get myself killed!*" The familiar scowl fell into place, and Pinchgutt added, "What kind of fool do you take me for, girl?"

"Not a fool," Beatrice said. She blew her bangs aside and looked squarely into Pinchgutt's hostile eyes. "We have a plan, but we need your help. You have a talent that would be useful to us."

Pinchgutt's eyes narrowed. "You mean walking through walls?"

"That's it," Beatrice replied. "You see, we know a way to enter the Treasure Room in Bailiwick Castle, but the room is probably locked from the outside. We need you to walk through the wall and find the key to unlock the door, allowing us to enter the rest of the castle."

"The Treasure Room," Pinchgutt muttered, looking off into space, and Beatrice could see that she had given him something to think about. But then his head jerked up, and he was glaring at her. "And just how do you figure on getting into the Treasure Room?" he demanded.

"We'll tell you that part after you've agreed to help us," Beatrice replied.

"Oh, you will, will you? How *generous* of you," Pinchgutt said sarcastically. "But just tell me this, Miss Got-It-All-Figured-Out Bailiwick, why should I risk my life to help *you?* Aside from me being a civic-minded gent, I mean. Plainly spoken, what's in it for me?"

Beatrice opened her mouth to tell him, but another voice beat her to it.

"Think about it, you numbskull!" Blacksheep Jones roared. He was sitting at a table behind Pinchgutt, looking disgusted. "Has it not occurred to you that you'll be in the same room with all that treasure? I'll wager there's more gold and silver there than either of us has seen in a lifetime."

"More than anyone has seen," Beatrice slipped in quickly, "even Wolf Duvall."

Blacksheep Jones looked at Beatrice with something close to admiration. "That's right," he said, turning his attention back to Pinchgutt. "Think of Wolf's reaction when he finds out you've actually made it inside the Treasure Room. Maybe you'd want to give him a ruby or two—as an act of charity, you might say."

A gleam came to Pinchgutt's eyes as he considered what the highwayman had just said. It was obvious that Pinchgutt had taken the bait. But Blacksheep Jones's booming voice had also captured the attention of nearly everyone else in the room. A sea of inquisitive eyes seemed to be focused on Pinchgutt's table.

"I think we should talk about this outside," Beatrice said quietly.

Blacksheep Jones glanced around at the curious faces and nodded. "Yes, let's take a walk."

No one had actually invited Blacksheep to participate in the discussion—or Ganef or Badger, either—but all three rose from their tables and accompanied Pinchgutt,

Beatrice, and her friends out of the tavern. The highwayman started down the street as if they had just stepped out for a leisurely stroll.

"So tell us," Blacksheep said to Beatrice, "how you intend to get inside the Treasure Room."

Beatrice hesitated. She hadn't expected to have to reveal the secret of the tunnels to so many people.

"Go ahead," Miranda prompted her. "We need their help."

So Beatrice told them quickly about the system of tunnels called Thieves' Lair, and how one tunnel led directly to the castle's Treasure Room.

"But how will you deal with all the goblins guarding the castle?" Badger asked.

"I know!" Ganef burst out, grinning. "You could go with them, Badge, and use your explosions to distract the guards."

"Not a bad idea," Blacksheep Jones murmured. Then he turned his gaze on Beatrice and she saw a glint of excitement in those dark eyes. "And *I* can create a diversion outside the castle," he said, "and keep some of the guards occupied there."

"Great!" Ganef exclaimed. "So what do you say, Badger?"

"It *would* be a job of a lifetime, wouldn't it?" Badger said, beginning to grin as he warmed up to the idea. "But what'll you do, Ganef?"

Ganef's face fell. "I hadn't thought about that," he admitted. "But I'd sure hate to be left out."

"You can ride with me, my boy," Blacksheep Jones said magnanimously. "We'll get you a horse as swift as the wind, a noble steed like the best of the highwaymen have."

Ganef's face glowed. "*All right!*"

"But that could be dangerous," Beatrice cut in, thinking how John Chew had been attacked on the road outside the castle. "Ganef, there's no reason for you to take the risk. Or you either, Badger."

"No reason except that we want to," Ganef said jauntily. "It's kind of you to worry about our safety, Beatrice, but have you forgotten what we are? We're *outlaws!*" he proclaimed with equal measures of pride and joy. "And the best part is the danger—the risks we take every day."

"Well said, my boy!" Blacksheep Jones grinned and slapped Ganef on the back.

"Badger's explosions *could* be a real help," Teddy said to Beatrice. "And with Blacksheep and Ganef creating a diversion outside . . ."

"What is it exactly that you intend to do?" Beatrice asked the highwayman.

"I was thinking about that," Blacksheep said. "There's a coach due in Heraldstone shortly after nine tonight. If you could leave this evening, my young friend and I could rob the coach right outside the castle."

"There's no reason we couldn't go tonight," Ollie said to Beatrice.

"But John Chew was attacked by goblins outside the castle," Beatrice said stubbornly. "I don't want Ganef to take that kind of risk."

"You have no need to worry about the boy," Blacksheep said calmly. "I'll be keeping an eye out for guards from the castle—and should any start for us, I'll whisk him away before they can raise their bows or draw their swords."

"Anyhow, it's not your place to tell me what I can and can't do," Ganef said, clearly unhappy with Beatrice now. "And I've decided to ride with Blacksheep Jones tonight."

Beatrice frowned at Ganef, who frowned right back. Then she turned to Badger, who said hastily, "And *I'm* going through the tunnels with Pinchgutt."

"Assuming Pinchgutt is going," Teddy said. She gave the thief an inquiring look. "Have you decided?" she asked.

"What choice do I have?" Pinchgutt grumbled. "I can't have these boys show me up, now, can I?"

But Beatrice knew that visions of gold and silver, diamonds and rubies, were the real reasons for Pinchgutt agreeing to go. It was that greed that troubled her. That, and the fact that Pinchgutt didn't feel an ounce of loyalty toward them. Could they depend on him? Might he run off with his pockets stuffed with treasure just when they needed him most? *Well*, Beatrice thought, *there's no way to know that until we enter the castle.*

"You should plan to be in the Treasure Room no later than 8:30," Blacksheep Jones was saying to Beatrice. He was all business now, his expression serious. "So figure out how long it will take you to get from Heraldstone to the castle, and then add some extra time for unexpected delays. The coach should pass by the castle a little before nine. That's when Ganef and I will play our part, and when you should leave the Treasure Room and start for the dungeon. Understand?"

149

"Wait a minute," Beatrice said. "You won't hurt anyone in that coach, will you? Because I can't agree to this if there's going to be violence."

Blacksheep rolled his eyes skyward. "No one will get hurt," he said testily. "Now—is there anything else troubling you?"

"Just one more thing," Beatrice said, ignoring the long-suffering look her gave her. "Why are *you* willing to take the risk to help us?"

Blacksheep Jones placed his arm around Ganef's shoulder. "It's just as my young friend here told you," Blacksheep said. "We're outlaws. And the danger is the very best part."

Pinchgutt and Badger were to meet Beatrice outside Wolf's house at 6:45. Then she would have the daunting task of smuggling them into the house and up to the secret closet without Wolf, Hobnob, or Ludwig seeing them. They would leave for the tunnels no later than seven.

"It looks like it's a straight shot to the castle," Beatrice said, studying the map spread out on her bed, "so we should be there before eight. But I think it's a good idea to give ourselves that extra half hour."

"What if the entrance to the Treasure Room *has* been sealed off?" Teddy asked. "Then Blacksheep's show with the coach will be for nothing."

"Pinchgutt could get into the Treasure Room by walking through the wall," Ollie said, "and maybe find a way to let us in."

"If he sticks around long enough," Miranda said bluntly. "I don't have a good feeling about this. We're depending on a bunch of *crooks*, for Pete's sake."

There was a sharp rap on the door, and Beatrice just had time to shove the map under her bed before Ludwig barged in with a stack of towels.

"You brought us towels this morning," Beatrice reminded the spriggan.

"So now you have more," he growled, and threw the towels on Miranda's bed.

After he had left, slamming the door behind him, Cyrus said softly, "I wonder if he heard anything we said."

"Obviously not," Teddy said, "or he wouldn't have had to use that lame excuse about bringing towels."

A few minutes later, there was another knock on the door. Beatrice opened it to find Hobnob filling the entire doorway.

"Mr. Duvall requests that you join him in his study after dinner," Hobnob said, black eyes glittering as they pierced Beatrice's face.

Beatrice was caught completely off guard. After dinner? They wouldn't *be here* after dinner.

"Mr. Duvall thought you might enjoy a game of cards. Thieves' Ransom, it's called." There was a change in Hobnob's grim expression that was very nearly a smirk.

"That sounds interesting," Ollie said smoothly. "What time should we be there?"

"He suggested 7:30," Hobnob said, "if that's convenient."

"Tell Mr. Duvall that we'll be looking forward to it," Ollie said pleasantly.

After she had closed the door, Beatrice walked over to the nearest bed and collapsed on it. "Thank goodness you were able to carry that off," she said to Ollie. "My mind went blank! I couldn't think how to respond without sounding guilty. But why, all of a sudden, is Wolf inviting us to play cards?"

"He knows we're leaving tonight," Miranda said. "He *has* to!"

"And how am I ever going to get Pinchgutt and Badger upstairs?" Beatrice demanded. "Trust me, the one time we don't want them around, Wolf and Hobnob and that obnoxious Ludwig will be all over the place."

"I think I have an idea," Cyrus said. He walked over to one of the beds and jerked off the blanket.

Beatrice met Pinchgutt and Badger down the block from Wolf's house and told them about the change of plans. A few minutes later, the thief and the pickpocket climbed up to the girls' room using a rope made from sheets taken off their beds.

"Brilliant idea," Beatrice said to Cyrus, who beamed.

Teddy peered out into the hall to make sure no one was there, and then Ollie led them all quickly to the hidden opening across from John Chew's closed door. He pushed open the panel and motioned for everyone to enter the closet.

With a flashlight in one hand, the map in the other, and Cayenne perched on her shoulder, Beatrice was the first to start down the narrow staircase. When they had all reached the closet adjoining Wolf's study, Beatrice pressed her ear to the wall and heard nothing. She figured Wolf must be at The Galloping Ghost having dinner. *If he doesn't already know what we're doing tonight,* Beatrice thought, *he'll certainly know when we don't show up for cards.* But by then, it would be too late for him to do anything about it. She *hoped.*

Beatrice and Miranda turned on their flashlights and directed them across the floor. *There it was—the trapdoor.* Ollie stooped, and pulling on the iron ring in the door, lifted it open. The old hinges squeaked a little, and Beatrice froze. But there was still no sound from the study.

The flight of stairs to the cellar was exactly like the one they had just come down. Flashing her light along the shallow steps, Beatrice was reassured to see that they were thick with dust that had been undisturbed for a long time. At least no one had come down here recently. Maybe not since Wolf's great-grandfather. Then Beatrice remembered that the man had met his end somewhere in these tunnels, and she decided to stop thinking for the moment.

She came to the bottom of the staircase and aimed her flashlight beam straight ahead. There was a wooden door with iron fittings. The others gathered around her, staring at the door.

Finally, Pinchgutt stepped forward and said gruffly, "I'll do the honors."

He took hold of the rusted handle and pulled. The door creaked open.

Beatrice shone a light inside. All she could see was a corridor no more than three feet wide, with dark walls, a dirt floor, and a curtain of cobwebs hanging from the ceiling. Her heart was thumping hard against her ribs. She really didn't want to go into this dark, tight space. But she had no choice.

Beatrice stepped through the door and into the tunnel. Walking slowly down the narrow passage, she glanced nervously over her shoulder to make sure that everyone else was behind her.

A cobweb fell across Beatrice's face, clinging like fine silk thread to her skin. She clawed it away, fighting the urge to turn around and run back upstairs.

Just ahead, in the flashlight's beam, Beatrice could see that the tunnel branched into three separate ones. She took a deep breath, trying to steady her nerves. They were about to enter the maze.

15

The Treasure Room

They stopped where the tunnel branched off in three different directions.

"Which one do we take?" Miranda asked.

Beatrice unrolled the map and held it close to the beam of the flashlight. "The center one," she said.

Every time they came to a place where tunnels intersected, or one branched off from another, they would have to wait for Beatrice to consult the map. After awhile, she began to doubt herself. There were so many passages—twisting and crossing and taking off in new directions. Had she missed any of the turns? Were they still heading toward the castle, or had she led them the wrong way? One mistake, and they could be lost down here forever.

They continued on, ducking under spiders' webs, stepping over chunks of crumbling stone that had fallen from the walls and ceiling, and Beatrice kept her worries to herself. Sometimes she heard faint scurrying sounds nearby and hoped that it was only mice.

They had just taken another turn when Beatrice saw a large, cavelike chamber illuminated by the flashlight's beam. There were piles of dust-covered straw and stubs of candles stuck into niches in the walls.

"This must have been where the thieves slept when they were in hiding," Ollie said.

"Not exactly four-star accommodations," Teddy said, peering uneasily into the shadowy cavern.

Just then, something large and black swooped out of the chamber and landed on Beatrice's head. In the next confused moments, she heard wings flapping and felt sharp claws digging into her scalp. Her screams echoed down the passage as she waved her arms wildly above her head, trying to fight off the creature clinging to her hair.

"It's a bat!" came Teddy's screeching voice, just as Cayenne leaped from the tunnel floor and knocked the animal to the ground.

Beatrice stumbled and fell to her knees as the bat sailed down the passage and disappeared. Cayenne climbed into Beatrice's lap and stared up into her mistress's face with concern.

"Cayenne," Beatrice said weakly, gathering the cat up into her arms. "You've helped me again. You're such a brave, wonderful girl."

"Beatrice, you're bleeding," Ollie said.

Crouching down beside her, he began dabbing gently at Beatrice's temple with a handkerchief. His face was so close to hers, Beatrice could see three faint freckles beneath his left eye, something she had never noticed before. And in the glow from her flashlight, she saw that his long, dark lashes were actually tipped with gold.

Beatrice dropped her eyes, her heart beating fast. Before she had time to think about the reason for this,

Cyrus said in a worried voice, "You're going to need a tetanus shot, Beatrice."

"What's a tet—whatever you said?" Pinchgutt demanded, looking perplexed. "It was just a bat."

Ollie stood up, and Beatrice felt a twinge of disappointment. Then she caught sight of Pinchgutt's bewildered face, which struck her as funny, and she started to giggle.

"That's the spirit," Pinchgutt said encouragingly.

"It *was* kind of humorous," Badger said with a grin. "Beatrice, you were waving your hands around like a crazy person—and not coming anywhere near that bat!"

"If you're okay," Miranda said to Beatrice, trying not to sound too impatient, "we'd better get going."

"I'm fine," Beatrice said, struggling to her feet and placing Cayenne on her shoulder.

They started down the tunnel again, and a few minutes later, it was Teddy's turn to scream.

"It was a rat," Teddy said defensively when Miranda gave her a disgusted look. "It ran right over my foot." She shuddered. "What else are we going to run into down here?"

"If it's only bats and rats," Pinchgutt muttered, "you can consider yourself lucky."

The wound on Beatrice's head was stinging a little and her nerves were raw. Every faint sound—the scurrying of some small creature, the scrape of a shoe sole against stone—caused her to catch her breath sharply. But she wasn't about to whine or act scared in front of Pinchgutt and Badger.

Beatrice had just rounded a sharp corner in the tunnel when her foot struck something. She glanced down, expecting to see more crumbling stone—and froze. In the beam of light on the tunnel floor was a skeleton! A human skull, arms, long bony fingers—and there, in the rib cage, was a knife with a broad, curved blade.

Beatrice was too horrified to utter a sound. It was Pinchgutt who emitted a shocked oath, and then muttered, "*Now* you've got something to worry about."

Ollie and Badger were bending over the skeleton.

"These bones are real old," Badger said.

"His clothes have disintegrated," Ollie added, "but you can still see scraps of cloth."

Pinchgutt reached down and picked up a rotting piece of dusty blue fabric. "Silk," he muttered. "This wasn't a poor man, dressed like that. He was a gentleman."

"A gentleman stabbed in the heart," Badger said.

"I wonder," Beatrice said slowly, her eyes still locked on the knife, "if this could be Wolf's great-grandfather, Sam Hill Duvall."

Pinchgutt grunted. "They say he never came back from robbing Bailiwick Castle."

"Do you think Dally Rumpe's goblins got him?" Ollie asked.

"If they did," Pinchgutt said, "then we must be nearing the castle."

Everyone was subdued as they started out again. Beatrice couldn't get the image of the knife stuck into that poor man's ribs out of her mind. She glanced at her watch.

"It's 8:15."

"So we have about forty minutes till Blacksheep attacks the coach," Miranda said.

"I wonder how much farther to the Treasure Room," Teddy murmured.

"Not far," Beatrice replied, and came to a stop.

Her flashlight beam was resting on a set of shallow stone steps a few yards ahead. The steps led to an old wooden door, very much like the one they had come through to reach the tunnels.

Beatrice felt a shiver dart down her spine. So they had finally made it to the castle. She glanced at Pinchgutt, expecting to see excitement in his face now that they were so close to the treasure. But the thief was just staring at the door. Beatrice thought she detected fear in his strained expression.

Turning back to the door, Beatrice blew her bangs out of her eyes and started toward the steps. She heard the others following, but she kept her eyes on the wooden door, climbing the steps slowly and then reaching out to grab the iron handle.

Beatrice tugged, but the door wouldn't open.

Miranda looked at Pinchgutt and said, "It's time for you to do your stuff."

Pinchgutt didn't move for a moment, but then he became aware of everyone's eyes on him, and frowned. "All right," he said gruffly. "Give me room."

"Take this," Ollie said, handing Pinchgutt his flashlight.

The thief climbed the steps until he was standing beside Beatrice. He focused on the door, and then, suddenly, he was walking through it.

The others watched in astonishment as Pinchgutt disappeared through the thick wood, as easily as if he had just stepped into a bank of clouds.

"Incredible," Teddy whispered.

The waiting seemed interminable, but then Pinchgutt's head appeared through the closed door, and he said, "I don't see an entrance on this side, but I'll keep looking for it. And this *is* the Treasure Room, all right." His dark eyes gleamed with greedy pleasure. "You wouldn't believe all the gold in here. Not to mention the rubies and emeralds."

"Just find a door," Miranda snapped, "and we'll see it for ourselves."

Pinchgutt's head vanished, and Beatrice and the others waited again. Minutes passed and the thief didn't reappear. Beatrice was beginning to think that he had just stuffed his pockets full of treasure and gone out another way, not intending to let them in. But then she heard a scraping sound, and very slowly, the old wooden door began to open.

Cayenne leaped from Beatrice's shoulder and trotted through the doorway. Beatrice was right behind her, and the others were hurrying up the steps to join them.

Beatrice's first impression was of a large, shadowy room filled with trunks and piles of cloth bags. She aimed her flashlight behind the door, where Pinchgutt was standing, and saw that the back of the door appeared to be made of stone, as were the walls. With the entrance closed, she imagined that it would be impossible to find the opening without knowing where to look for it.

"Can you believe all this?" Pinchgutt demanded.

Beatrice looked around, as did her companions, and they were too overwhelmed to utter a word. There must have been fifty or more large trunks, their domed lids open so that their contents was clearly visible. Heaps of gold coins were in some, jeweled bracelets and necklaces and other ornaments in others. And then there were chests that held loose emeralds or diamonds or rubies. Beatrice's eyes lingered on the rubies. No doubt these glowing red stones had come from the Bailiwick Ruby Mines on Blood Mountain.

Then Beatrice's eyes darted to the shadowy corners of the room. No one seemed to be hiding; there were just piles of cloth bags stacked up nearly to the ceiling.

"What's in those bags?" Beatrice asked Pinchgutt.

"Silver," he answered, holding up a bag that he had slit with his knife and withdrawing a silver coin.

"I knew Bromwich was rich," Cyrus said in a hushed voice, "but I had no idea he was *this* rich."

"It all belongs to Dally Rumpe now," Badger said darkly.

"But not for long," Miranda declared.

She walked quickly to a door on the other side of the room and tried to open it. Turning back to the others, she shook her head. "It's locked," she said.

They had all been speaking softly, but Beatrice doubted that anyone could have heard them through these thick stone walls even if they had been shouting.

Still, she kept her voice low when she said to Pinchgutt, "You'll have to walk through the door and see if it opens from the other side. If not, you'll need to find a key."

Pinchgutt scowled at her. "I'll wager there's goblins outside that door," he said, "and I don't fancy ending up like that gent we saw in the tunnels."

"But you promised to help us get into the other part of the castle," Teddy reminded him sternly.

"Wait a minute, Teddy," Beatrice said. "He's right. There probably *are* guards out there. We can't force him to take that risk. It's Pinchgutt's decision whether he helps us or not."

"Of course he'll help you!" Badger exclaimed, grinning at the older thief. "You've never been scared of anything, have you, Pinchgutt? And you've had some pretty close calls. It'll take more than a few goblins to make you run."

Pinchgutt's scowl deepened as he stared hard at his eager young friend. "All right," he growled. Then, squaring his broad shoulders, he walked quickly through the stone wall.

After a few moments, when Pinchgutt didn't stick his head back inside, Beatrice began to grow nervous. More time passed, and she started to feel really afraid. Even Badger's confidence had waned, and he began to pace back and forth, looking worried.

"They got him," Badger muttered, "and it's my fault. He would've felt like a coward if he'd refused."

"It isn't your fault," Beatrice said hastily.

But then they heard a creaking sound, and the old door opened. Pinchgutt stepped through the doorway, his face pale under all the grime, and his jaw tight as if he were gritting his teeth.

"There's a corridor outside lit with torches," he whispered. "I didn't see anyone, but they're probably close by. Dally Rumpe's not likely to leave his treasures unguarded, now, is he?"

Beatrice touched Pinchgutt's arm gently. "That was a brave thing to do, and we're very grateful."

Badger's grin had returned, and he slapped Pinchgutt heartily on the back.

"Well," Pinchgutt said grimly, "I kept my word. I got you into the Treasure Room and gave you a way to reach the rest of the castle. But this is as far as I go."

"You can't mean that," Badger said cheerfully. "You don't want to miss all the action, do you?"

"I said, I'm leaving," Pinchgutt snapped. "I'll just take a few choice items from these stores, and no one will ever miss them."

Beatrice realized that she didn't want him to go. Besides his unusual talent, which had proved invaluable, the thief's presence gave her a feeling of security. But he had kept his promise, and she had no intention of asking more of him.

"Leave the door into the tunnels open," Beatrice said to Pinchgutt, "just in case we have to get out of here fast. And thank you for everything you've done."

Pinchgutt nodded. Then he looked Beatrice straight in the eye and burst out, "Why do you want to end up dead, anyhow? You aren't such bad kids, not anything like what I expected. Why don't you all help yourselves to a few baubles and leave with me?"

Beatrice smiled. She bet this was the closest Pinchgutt would ever come to paying them a compliment. "You know we can't do that," she said.

"All right," the thief said gruffly, "suit yourself. And *you*," he said to Badger, "it's been nice knowing you. I expect I won't be seeing you again."

"I wouldn't count on that," Badger said stoutly. But he appeared uncertain as he watched Pinchgutt scoop up jewels and gold pieces and cram them into his pockets.

Pinchgutt gave them one last unreadable look before striding to the door that led to the tunnels and disappearing from sight.

"You can go with him if you want to," Beatrice said to Badger.

"And leave you high and dry?" the boy demanded. "Not likely. Besides, I haven't gotten to make even one explosion yet."

"Well," Beatrice said, looking around at all their faces, "is everyone ready?"

They all nodded, and Beatrice started through the doorway. Badger hurried after her. "You may need me up front when we run into the goblins," he said.

"I'm sure I will," Beatrice agreed.

They found themselves in a long, empty corridor. Lit torches every few feet cast fitful shadows on the stone walls. The air was freezing and Beatrice shivered. Remembering Cayenne, she looked around for the cat.

"Come on," Beatrice said softly, and Cayenne leaped to her shoulder.

They came to a turn in the corridor, and Beatrice motioned for everyone to stop. Then she peered cautiously around the corner. A few feet away was a large alcove containing a table and two straight-back chairs. And sitting at the table, playing cards, were two of the most ghastly creatures Beatrice had ever seen!

Pale and bald, their masklike faces seemed drained of blood, as well as expression. Their mouths were no more than thin lines stretched in a grim path from ear to ear, their eyes were mere slits that gleamed silver, and they had no noses at all. They were tall—*how* tall Beatrice couldn't tell since they were seated—and bone thin. The long white hands protruding from the sleeves of their dark blue tunics resembled those of the skeleton in the tunnel. Beatrice's gaze fell to the swords they wore at their waists. The creatures had to be Dally Rumpe's goblins.

Beatrice took a step back, but one of the goblins must have seen the movement because his head jerked up—and those narrow silver eyes glinted as they landed on Beatrice's face.

In an instant, both goblins had leaped to their feet and reached for their swords.

16

Out of the Mouths of Goblins

"**B**adger!" Beatrice screamed.

The two goblins moved swiftly to the front of the alcove, prepared to charge into the hallway at the intruders. Badger raised one arm and pointed an index finger in the guards' direction. Suddenly, the torch above the goblins' heads exploded with a thundering *boom*, sending a spray of fire into the air, while dense clouds of black smoke billowed out into the corridor.

Beatrice could no longer see the goblins for the smoke, but she could hear them shrieking, then coughing and gasping. With Cayenne clinging to her shoulder, Beatrice raced down the corridor past the goblins, blinded by the smoke, eyes burning and tearing as she emerged on the other side. Badger and the others were right behind her.

"Fantastic job!" Beatrice exclaimed to the young thief, then added quickly, "Let's get out of here!"

They ran the length of the corridor, with Beatrice looking back once and seeing only smoke. She barreled around the corner, trying to think while they put distance between themselves and the goblins. She was pretty sure they were on a floor beneath the castle—maybe the same floor as the dungeon. But which direction should they go? The castle was huge. It could take hours to find Bromwich, and they didn't have hours. She was sure that other castle guards had heard the torch explode and would be coming to investigate.

Beatrice was turning her head from left to right as they ran, looking for anything that might show them the way to the dungeon, when suddenly, she felt a heavy hand clamp down on her shoulder.

Beatrice spun around, ready to kick and claw for her life—but it wasn't a goblin behind her. It was Pinchgutt!

"You came back," Beatrice said in astonishment. "But why? And how did you get past—"

"The smoke?" Pinchgutt finished with a growl. "It nearly put my eyes out! But it kept the goblins from seeing me. They were bent over, choking and slapping each other on the back, when I slipped past."

"But what are you doing here?" Miranda demanded, wiping the tears from her own reddened eyes.

"Well, you had to have *somebody*," Pinchgutt muttered. "You're all such innocents! I don't know how you get through a day alive."

Beatrice didn't care that he was insulting them. She didn't care *why* he had come back. She was just glad to see him!

"We're trying to find the dungeon," she told him.

"And we'd better get moving," Ollie said, "before those goblins recover."

At that moment, Beatrice saw a wide stone staircase just ahead—and galloping down the stairs, with swords and daggers raised, were at least a dozen more goblins. Beatrice froze. They couldn't turn back. They were trapped!

"Listen up!" Pinchgutt shouted. "Everybody hold hands. Form a chain," he ordered, and grabbed for Beatrice's hand.

There was no time to question what he intended to do, and he spoke with such authority that everyone obeyed. The next thing Beatrice knew, Pinchgutt was jerking her arm with so much force he nearly pulled it out of its socket—and then—*surely not!*—yes, he was yanking her through one of the stone walls! The others followed them through the wall, resembling a human whip.

Everyone looked stunned for a moment, and then—when it dawned on them what Pinchgutt had done—they grinned and began to congratulate the thief.

Pinchgutt, however, seemed unaware of the accolades as he wiped his forehead on his sleeve and exhaled deeply.

"I wasn't sure that would work," he admitted hoarsely. "I've never pulled anyone else through a wall with me."

"This is a fine time to experiment," Miranda quipped.

"Well, *pardon me*," Pinchgutt shot back. "I didn't realize that you'd rather be on the end of a goblin's sword."

"Where are we, anyway?" Ollie asked, looking around.

They were in a large room filled with barrels and bulging sacks. Jars and crockery lined shelves on the walls.

"It's the pantry," Pinchgutt said. "The kitchen must be through that door."

"Maybe we can reach another corridor through the kitchen," Teddy said.

But then they heard footsteps—*many* footsteps—moving at a rapid pace toward the pantry door.

Pinchgutt's head jerked toward the sound. "Join hands," he barked.

Beatrice scooped up Cayenne again and reached for Pinchgutt's hand. Before she knew what was happening, he had pulled them through another wall.

Now they were in an empty corridor. Beatrice had no idea where they were in relation to the Treasure Room, much less the dungeon.

"So which way do we go?" she muttered.

"We could flip a coin," Miranda said. She cut her eyes at Pinchgutt. "You have some on you, I believe."

But before they could act, their decision was made for them. There was the sound of a door opening behind them. Beatrice and her companions spun around, just in time to see a lone goblin step from a doorway at the end of the corridor.

The goblin stopped short when he saw them. Then, reaching for his sword, he screeched in a voice that would break glass, "Halt, intruders! Come back at once. Away from the dungeon. *I repeat*, away from the dungeon!"

A lot of jumbled thoughts passed through Beatrice's mind at that moment, but paramount were these: The goblin would alert others that they were there—and he had just revealed the location of the dungeon!

Suddenly the goblin was joined by six or eight more, and they were racing down the passageway toward Beatrice and her companions. Badger and the others had already started to run. In desperation, Beatrice blurted out the first spell that occurred to her.

Circle of magic, hear my pleas,
Drop hailstones large
On our enemies.
This, I ask you, do for me.

All at once, hailstones the size of billiard balls began to fall on the goblins. The guards yelped and screamed and crouched to the floor, wrapping their long arms around their heads—too busy trying to dodge the onslaught to continue the chase.

Pinchgutt and the others had stopped running and turned around to see what all the commotion was.

"Now *that* little trick could be useful to a thief," Pinchgutt said, grinning at Beatrice.

Beatrice hadn't been sure it would work. She had never cast a weather spell indoors. But the hailstones continued to beat down on the goblins' heads, and Beatrice and her companions took off again down the corridor.

They turned a corner, and what Beatrice saw at the end of the long hall made her feel like cheering. There was a wide archway—and just beyond was what looked like a cell door, with thick iron bars from floor to ceiling.

"The dungeon!" Ollie exclaimed.

"It has to be," Cyrus added.

They were running as fast as they could. Beatrice was certain that in just a few moments she would finally meet Bromwich. They were going to make it!

But as they drew closer, something very strange appeared in the archway. Beatrice screeched to a stop, trying to identify what she was seeing. Creatures as fluid and diaphanous as ghosts were floating from the direction of the cells and through the arch. But unlike ghosts, the figures were the color of chimney soot, and their eyes—their eyes glowed like yellow coals, menacing and horrible! Then Beatrice remembered what Dr. Featherstone had told them.

"The Furies!" Beatrice shouted. "Their touch will kill you!"

Now the nightmarish creatures were speeding through the air toward the witches, emitting anguished, terrifying cries.

Beatrice's head was swimming. She knew there was no point in running. The Furies were too fast. They would follow. They would stretch out their filmy arms, and then—Beatrice could almost feel the creatures' deadly fingers trailing down her face. There was no way out this time. She was going to die!

17

The Furies

The Furies were directly over them, only feet above their heads, when Beatrice felt someone grab her arm. The next thing she knew, she was sailing through the wall, and then tumbling to the cold floor.

Beatrice looked around, feeling dazed. All her friends were lying beside her, with Badger sprawled on top of Pinchgutt.

"Get off me!" Pinchgutt bellowed, jerking his legs out from under the young pickpocket.

"You've done it again," Beatrice said weakly to Pinchgutt. "You saved us."

Pinchgutt just shook his head, and then he muttered, "Don't know how they make it through a day. Bunch of innocents!"

Everyone was scrambling to sit up while they looked around the room. It was huge, with an enormous fireplace and a long wooden table in the center.

"We're in the kitchen," Miranda said, getting to her feet. "So if we go out that door, and turn right at the first corner, we'll be back in the corridor that leads to the dungeon."

"*You* can go out that door," Teddy muttered, "but I'm staying right here till we're sure those Furies are gone."

"Maybe they *never* leave," Cyrus said. "Maybe they help Zortag guard Bromwich."

"It sure is quiet in here," Badger said, glancing furtively around the room.

Ollie walked over to the table, where several loaves of bread had been placed on pewter platters. He touched one of the loaves, and said, "It's still warm, so someone was here not long ago."

"And the floor's just been mopped," Beatrice said, looking across the wet stone floor at a pail filled with water.

Just then the door swung open. Beatrice and her companions tensed, preparing to run. But the woman who came into the kitchen looked anything but frightening.

She was small and appeared quite frail, wearing an apron over her neat gray robes, with her white hair twisted into a knot on top of her head. When she saw that the kitchen was filled with people, she looked startled—but then a smile came to her lips and her blue eyes regarded them kindly.

"You must be the witches everyone's searching for," the woman said. "Don't be afraid," she added quickly, when Badger started backing away. "I wouldn't think of turning you in."

"You work for Dally Rumpe, don't you?" Pinchgutt said gruffly.

"Against my will," she answered, her voice surprisingly strong. "I was one of Bromwich's cooks, and I live for the day when I can serve that good man again."

"Then maybe you could help us," Beatrice said. She wasn't sure she trusted the woman, but someone from inside the castle could give them all sorts of useful information.

"You're Beatrice Bailiwick, aren't you?" the woman said, looking pleased. "I've heard whispers about you for months now. You've come to break the evil sorcerer's spell."

"Yes," Beatrice said. "That's why we're here. But we have to find Bromwich."

"And we couldn't get near the dungeon because of those awful Furies," Cyrus said.

"Ah, the Furies," the woman said softly. "They're deadly creatures."

Beatrice was eager to ask her if there was another way to the dungeon, but then she noticed something odd— and the words died in her throat. The woman's eyes were changing color. Beatrice watched, first in bewilderment, then with growing horror, as the woman's eyes turned from pale blue to yellow, as they began to glow, as the gentle face and the neat robes seemed to grow dim—and then turn filmy and soot colored.

"Oh, my gosh!" Teddy shouted. "She's one of them!"

The old woman-turned-Fury was laughing as she floated into the air, and one of her wispy hands reached out for Beatrice.

Beatrice stepped back. Still laughing, the Fury pursued her, but slowly, as if playing a game of cat and mouse. Cayenne was struggling in Beatrice's arms, hissing and baring her claws at the ghastly phantom. Beatrice was trying so hard to hold on to the furious cat, she barely noticed at first that Ollie was saying something. Then she caught the final words of his chant.

> Boil this water, bubbling free,
> As my will, so mote it be!

Beatrice glanced sharply at Ollie and saw that he was hurrying across the room, carrying the pail of water. Then he was beside her, flinging the boiling water into the Fury's face.

The creature's laughter changed instantly to an agonized scream. It jerked back, flailing and shrieking. And then, as they all watched in shock and relief, the Fury floated to the floor and began to dissolve—until it was nothing more than a black, oily puddle.

"Come on," Ollie said softly, "before more goblins come in here and find us."

The others followed him into the pantry. Ollie shut the door behind them and leaned against it, breathing hard.

"Now we're trapped," Miranda said, her voice sounding on the edge of panic.

"Not with Pinchgutt here," Ollie said. "We don't need a door to get out."

"Oh," Miranda said. "Right."

"And we couldn't go out into the hall," Teddy added. "Those other Furies are probably waiting for us."

Everyone just stood there, looking blankly at one another.

"So what do we do?" Cyrus asked finally.

"I think we should stay right here for the time being," Pinchgutt said. "They'll search all around the dungeon and not find us—and maybe they'll start looking in another part of the castle."

"Yeah, like in here," Cyrus said darkly.

"I need to think," Beatrice said, beginning to pace around the room. "Cyrus could shrink us. We'd be harder to see that way."

"And move at a snail's pace," Teddy pointed out. "I think I'd rather stay my normal size."

"Listen!" Ollie said suddenly. "What's that noise?"

They all stood very still, listening. Beatrice could hear a faint scratching, very much like the sound Cayenne made when she ran across a wood floor after her catnip mouse.

"It's coming from over there," Badger said, "behind those barrels in the corner."

Beatrice and Ollie were closest, so they went over to look.

"It sounds like mice," Teddy said, "or maybe rats. Yuck!"

Ollie moved a large sack of flour out of the way, and Beatrice peered into the dark corner. She got a quick look at something darting between barrels—something covered with gray fur and bigger than Cayenne—and then she realized that the whole corner was swarming with—what? They had long tails and pointed faces like rats, and sharp, beady eyes—but they were huge!

Beatrice stepped back quickly. "You aren't going to like this, Teddy," she said.

"Rats?" Teddy asked, and shuddered. "I knew it! I'm not staying in here with those hideous things!"

But Teddy had no idea what hideous was until one of the giant rodents suddenly ran out from behind the barrels and dashed directly for her.

Teddy was so astonished, her scream was reduced to a peep, and she leaped with the agility of a gymnast onto the top of a crate. But now more of the rats were shooting out from their corner, and they seemed to be running deliberately toward the witches. Ollie kicked at one and it bared teeth as large as a beaver's. Ollie jumped aside, barely missing a bite in the ankle.

"They're attacking us!" Miranda cried. "What if they're enchanted?"

"Do you think their bite could be poisonous?" Cyrus asked breathlessly from atop a barrel.

Rats were running all over the room, their long hairless tails whipping around like angry snakes. Everyone had climbed up off the floor, but some of the rodents were standing on their hind legs now, nipping at the witches' feet. Beatrice was looking down at the rats from a stack of filled flour sacks and having a terrible time holding on to Cayenne, who was squirming to free herself from her mistress's arms.

"Forget it!" Beatrice said to the cat. "I know you want to help us, but you've gone after rats before—and nearly lost. And they weren't *half* this big."

"Blow them up!" Teddy screeched at Badger. "Make them explode!"

"But maybe they aren't enchanted at all," Cyrus said. "Maybe they're just very big rats. I hate to see you kill innocent animals."

"*Innocent!*" Miranda stormed. "That one just bit through my shoe! Come on, Badger—*do* something!"

Badger pointed his finger toward the corner where many of the rats were still scurrying around. Suddenly a large sack of flour exploded, sending sparks and a billowing cloud of white dust into the air. The rats immediately dashed for cover behind the barrels.

With Cayenne still struggling and growling in her arms, Beatrice said wearily, "You guys can stay if you want to, but I'm getting out of here."

"So am I," Teddy said emphatically, already hurrying for the door.

There was no sign of goblins or Furies in the kitchen, just the black puddle in the middle of the floor. Everyone skirted around it, trying not to look, and went to the door that opened into the hallway.

Badger stuck his head out, looked both ways, and said, "I don't see anything."

They stepped into the corridor and started toward the end with the archway. But they had taken only a few steps when they heard scuffling behind them. No one was surprised when they turned around and saw a slew of goblins coming around the corner.

The goblins were practically on top of Beatrice and the others—only this time they held long hunting bows. And aimed directly at the witches were a dozen flaming arrows.

18

Finally . . . the Dungeon

Beatrice heard Miranda mutter, "My turn."

Then Miranda spit out a chant so quickly that Beatrice barely caught the words.

> *Spirit of the earth and sea,*
> *This, I ask you, do for me;*
> *Take bows and arrows from their hands,*
> *So they won't work as the goblins planned.*

Instantly, the bows and the fire-tipped arrows were ripped from the guards' hands and went hurtling into the air. Flaming arrows were falling all around the goblins, who covered their heads and took off down the corridor away from Beatrice and her companions.

"Good work," Beatrice said to her cousin.

"That's a make-things-not-work spell, isn't it?" Badger said with a grin for Miranda. "There used to be an old robber in Heraldstone who could do that."

"But it's not going to hold the goblins back for long," Teddy said. "Let's stop talking and get moving."

They ran down the hall and through the wide archway. There was no sign of the Furies, or of anyone else. A few yards in front of them was a stone wall, with three doors made of thick iron bars that were rusted with age.

This is it, Beatrice thought, her knees suddenly feeling weak. All their trips to the Sphere had led to this moment: to finding Bromwich.

Beatrice walked toward the first cell. Through the bars, she could see windowless stone walls, stained where water had trickled down from the ceiling. Rusty chains with manacles attached were bolted to one wall above a pile of straw. But there was no one in the cell. It felt to Beatrice as if no life had existed here for a long time. There was just eery silence all around them.

"Maybe this isn't the right dungeon," Cyrus said in a small voice.

"Let's check the other cells," Ollie said.

He and Beatrice ran to the second barred door, with the others following close behind.

And there he was!

Slumped against the far wall, his face pressed into his drawn-up knees, was a man so emaciated and still that for a moment Beatrice thought she was seeing a skeleton. His black hair was streaked with gray and fell in a tangle past his shoulders. He was wearing a ragged shirt and trousers that were so filthy it was impossible to identify their original color. His feet and hands were gray with embedded dirt. Then Beatrice noticed chains leading from the wall to his bony, manacled wrists. The chains were so short he wouldn't even be able to stand, much less move around the cell.

They were so shocked by what they saw, no one could speak for a moment. And the man didn't move, his face still hidden against his knees, as if unaware of their presence. *Maybe he's asleep*, Beatrice thought, unwilling to even consider another reason for his stillness.

"Bromwich," Beatrice said softly, "we're here to help you."

The man didn't respond, and Beatrice felt a whisper of fear run through her body.

"Bromwich!" Beatrice repeated sharply.

A small sound, hardly louder than a sigh, came from the man. Then slowly, slowly, he lifted his head.

A long, gray-streaked beard covered the lower part of his face, but Beatrice could still see the deep hollows under his cheekbones and the eyes sunken back into their sockets. He appeared dazed, his eyes unfocused, but then a small spark of life seemed to return, and his gaze came to rest on Beatrice's face.

Now that she was looking straight into his eyes, Beatrice was startled. The eyes were gray, so pale they were almost silver. She was looking into Miranda's eyes.

Beatrice glanced at her cousin. There was no sign of impatience in Miranda's face now, but rather a look so tender and pained it brought a lump to Beatrice's throat.

Turning back to Bromwich, Beatrice said gently, "I'm Beatrice Bailiwick, and this," she added, taking her cousin's hand, "is Miranda Pengilly. We're both Bailiwicks, and we and our friends have come to break Dally Rumpe's spell."

Something flickered in his eyes, and Beatrice knew that he had heard her and understood. His head fell back weakly against the wall, his eyes still pinned to her face. Then his lips began to move, but no words came out.

"Don't try to speak yet," Beatrice said quickly. "I'm going to repeat the counterspell."

But Bromwich's body jerked as he tried to sit up straighter, and in a hoarse, quivering voice, barely above a whisper, he said, "My daughters."

"They're safe," Miranda answered. "Beatrice and her friends have broken the spells on the rest of Bailiwick, and your daughters are free."

Bromwich let out a long sigh. Then the corners of his mouth lifted, and he gave them a smile of such profound happiness that Beatrice felt tears spring to her eyes.

"And we're going to free you now," Beatrice said.

Bromwich nodded, seeming stronger. Beatrice could see the determination in his face. But then he frowned suddenly, and his eyes darted past Beatrice.

"Zortag," Bromwich said.

"He isn't here," Beatrice assured him.

"He . . . will be," Bromwich responded, his voice steadier now. "We need . . . to leave."

Beatrice glanced at Ollie. The counterspell was a long one. *Would* it be better to take Bromwich to a safer place before repeating it to him?

Ollie's face showed an instant of indecision, but then he said, "Let's get him out of there."

"But how?" Bromwich asked, leaning toward them earnestly now. "Zortag has the keys."

"Cyrus," Beatrice said, looking at her friend, "can you shrink us real fast so we can slip through the bars? Then you can shrink Bromwich and get him out of those chains."

"There's no need for all of us to go," Cyrus said. "I can do it quicker on my own."

"Then do it!" Miranda urged him.

Cyrus began to chant as fast as he could.

> By the mysteries, one and all,
> Make me shrink from tall to small.
> Cut me down to inches three,
> As my will, so mote it be.

Instantly, Cyrus began to shrink smaller and smaller, until he was only three inches tall. Pinchgutt and Badger were staring in astonishment at the tiny witch, but Cyrus was already running between the bars into Bromwich's cell.

"Hey, that spell's better than mine," Badger muttered.

Cyrus hurried over to Bromwich and placed his hand on the sorcerer's foot. "This will just take a minute," Cyrus said.

But before he had even begun the chant, Bromwich's head jerked up.

"Zortag," Bromwich said, his voice filled with dread. "I hear him coming." His eyes darted to Cyrus, and then to the others. "Run—before he sees you! And whatever you do, don't look into his eye!"

But it was already too late. They heard the echo of heavy footsteps—and then the monster appeared in the archway.

Zortag was at least seven feet tall, and even bonier than Bromwich, wearing ragged robes the color of gunmetal. His skin and the stringy hair falling into his face were the same deep gray. Beatrice had the impression of a long beaked nose, an oily sheen to his face—and that one enormous red eye in the center of his forehead, like a nasty boil ready to erupt. But she turned away quickly so that she wouldn't be looking directly into that eye. The eye that could paralyze them.

"Look away!" she yelled to the others.

Zortag moved slowly toward them. Beatrice could feel the air grow colder as he approached.

"So you've finally been found," the monster said in a deep, icy voice.

It was a voice that sounded dead, sending a shiver down Beatrice's spine. Cutting her eyes sideways, she could see the frosty clouds of breath from his mouth as he spoke.

"You've caused no end of trouble for everyone," Zortag continued. "For me, most of all. I've had to keep my roasting fire going all night—waiting for your arrival."

He took another step toward them, and Beatrice saw her companions cringe. They all looked terrified, even Pinchgutt. But then her eyes fell on Bromwich, who was hiding Cyrus with his hand, and she realized that Bromwich wasn't frightened at all. There wasn't a sign of weakness in his face. In fact, his gray eyes appeared as hard as the stone walls that imprisoned him, and his expression was angry and defiant.

"*You!*" Zortag said loudly. "Beatrice Bailiwick! Look at me."

Beatrice's body began to tremble, but she wouldn't look away from Bromwich's face. The fighting spirit was still there in his eyes, after all he had been through. An eternity of this horror! Beatrice could feel Bromwich's strength begin to seep into her bones.

Zortag took another step toward her. Beatrice forced herself not to flinch. Her back stiffened and she stood there without moving, still looking at Bromwich, feeling the connection with him grow deeper.

But out of the corner of her eye, Beatrice could see one of Zortag's hands. It looked like gray bones, with gnarled fingers and curved, pointed nails that resembled a vulture's talons. And he was gripping something in that hand. It was a long metal stick. A skewer. Beatrice realized that this was what the monster would use to roast them—turning them slowly over a blazing fire on that skewer.

Suddenly Beatrice felt light-headed. She was afraid she was going to faint. But Bromwich's eyes were burning into hers, and she could almost hear his thoughts urging her not to give up. *Stay strong, Beatrice Bailiwick! Fight him. Fight him!*

"You *will* obey me," Zortag said in that chilling voice.

Then Beatrice saw his empty hand reach for her, and she felt the sharp talons sink into her shoulder. It was like tiny knives stabbing through her skin to the bone.

Beatrice couldn't help herself. Her eyes fell from Bromwich's face, and she screamed!

19

A Second Prisoner

he monster's talons sank deeper into Beatrice's shoulder, and intense pain shot down her arm. Through the pain, Beatrice heard someone yell, "Let go of her!" And at the same moment, she saw something small and dark sail past her eyes toward Zortag. *It was Cayenne!*

Beatrice's head jerked toward the cat—and she saw with horror that Cayenne was clinging to the monster's face, raking the hideous gray skin with her claws. Blood was pouring—not red, but the color of tar—splashing onto Cayenne's coat and Beatrice's arm. The monster was shrieking in pain, puffs of frosty breath leaving icy crystals on Cayenne's long fur.

Zortag lurched back, withdrawing his claws from Beatrice's shoulder. She whipped around to face him—just in time to see him strike out at her cat, sending Cayenne flying into the bars of Bromwich's cell.

Beatrice ran to the crumpled heap of fur, screaming Cayenne's name, but the cat was already rising to her feet, fur standing out, green-gold eyes huge and outraged. She looked ready to charge at the monster again, but Beatrice grabbed her and held the cat's rigid body against her chest.

Zortag was still shrieking. Watching him covertly to avoid staring into that red eye, Beatrice saw thick black blood still streaming down his face and the front of his tattered robes. She also saw Badger kneeling beside the monster, pointing his finger at Zortag. Beatrice's heart leaped with hope, but the creature was too fast for the boy. He grabbed Badger with both hands and raised him high above his head, as if the young pickpocket were as light as a bag of goose down.

Ollie and Pinchgutt lunged at Zortag at the same moment. The monster staggered, but he didn't loosen his grip on Badger. Then Miranda crouched down behind the creature and pressed against the back of his legs, making him lose his balance. Still clutching her furious, squirming cat, Beatrice watched as Zortag toppled over Miranda's back and crashed to the floor. Badger was flung into the air and landed on top of the monster.

Zortag had hit his head on the stone floor and was barely conscious. Beatrice knew they had to restrain him, but that was going to be hard if they had to keep their eyes averted. Then she had an idea.

"Miranda, give me your scarf," Beatrice said.

Miranda untied the scarf at her neck without asking any questions, and handed it to her cousin. Edging over to the moaning monster, Beatrice knelt down and tied the scarf around his forehead, covering the eye.

"Cyrus, get Bromwich out of there," Ollie called, "before this thing comes to again."

Cyrus chanted his spell, and as Bromwich grew smaller, the manacles fell from his wrists.

"Bromwich, can you walk?" Beatrice asked.

The sorcerer, who was now the same size as Cyrus, nodded. "I'm sure I can," he said.

Beatrice watched as he took a few wobbly steps, and then, leaning against Cyrus, walked through the bars to freedom.

"This is astounding," Bromwich said to Beatrice. "All of you are absolutely amazing."

"We're not out of here yet," Beatrice answered, and then she noticed Zortag beginning to thrash around. "We need to tie him up or something," she muttered. Then it came to her; she knew *exactly* how to take care of Zortag.

"Cyrus," Beatrice said, "shrink him while he's still groggy, and we'll lock him up in Bromwich's cell."

"Good idea," Ollie said.

While Cyrus was chanting his spell—touching the monster's toe with a grimace—Ollie searched Zortag's robes. "No keys here," he said.

"That's all right," Beatrice replied as she cuddled Cayenne, who seemed fully recovered now from her battle with the one-eyed monster. "We don't need them."

When Zortag was reduced to Cyrus's size, Ollie picked up the miniature monster and pushed him through the bars into the cell. Then he shoved him hard across the floor, with Zortag ending up lying next to the chains that had bound Bromwich.

Cyrus ran through the bars to the monster. "Shall I put the manacles on him, too?" Cyrus asked.

"Definitely," Beatrice said.

In less than two minutes, Cyrus had returned Zortag to his normal size, with the manacles clamped around his wrists, and had slipped back through the bars. As the dazed Zortag groaned and struggled against the handcuffs, Miranda's scarf still covering his eye, Cyrus made Bromwich and himself big again.

Bromwich was leaning against the wall, looking exhausted after all this unaccustomed activity. But he was beaming at the faces around him.

"Now, I have to repeat the spell," Beatrice said, "before any more goblins arrive."

"The goblins never come back to the cells," Bromwich said. "They're terrified of Zortag. And they have no way of knowing that he's—*indisposed*," the sorcerer added with a grim, but gratified, glance at the imprisoned monster. Then he turned back abruptly to Beatrice, as if he had just thought of something. "Before you repeat the counterspell, you should take a look in the next cell. Zortag brought another prisoner in a little while ago."

"Do you know who it is?" Ollie asked.

Bromwich shook his head. "I just heard goblins out in the corridor telling Zortag that Dally Rumpe had a second prisoner, and that he wasn't to be harmed because Dally Rumpe might need him alive later. Then the goblins left quickly—probably quaking in their boots being that close to my jailer—and Zortag carried an unconscious man past my cell door. I couldn't see much—just an inert body in his arms. But if he's an enemy of Dally Rumpe's," Bromwich said, "we have to help him."

"Of course," Beatrice said, and went with the others to the last cell door.

"I can't believe it," Teddy gasped, and Pinchgutt uttered an oath under his breath.

Beatrice was too shocked to say anything. The second prisoner was shackled to the wall, just as Bromwich had been, his head dropped forward so that they couldn't see his face. But Beatrice would have known that shaggy thatch of dark hair and the blue tunic anywhere. It was Ganef!

"How do you suppose they got him?" Pinchgutt asked angrily. "He's smart and he's quick. I'd have thought he would have taken off in a second when he saw goblins coming."

"Well, John Chew didn't get away, either," Ollie said.

"They might have hit him with an arrow," Miranda added. "There's blood on the arm of his shirt."

Beatrice noticed that blood was matted in the boy's hair, as well. It looked like someone had hit him over the head.

"We have to get him out of there," Beatrice said. Then she said louder, "Ganef? It's Beatrice Bailiwick. Hold on, we're going to help you."

At the sound of her voice, Ganef lifted his head. They could see his face now, one side swollen and bruised, the other side covered with blood from the scalp wound. He appeared barely conscious, his head bobbing as he tried to speak. A jumble of words came out of his mouth that Beatrice didn't understand.

"It's okay, Ganef," she said. "Cyrus, can you shrink yourself again and get him out?"

"Sure," Cyrus answered.

Then Beatrice thought of something else. "I wonder if they got Blacksheep Jones, too."

"If they did—" Ollie stopped, frowning. "Well, they didn't bring him here."

"You mean, he's dead," Badger said, looking stricken. "Old Blacksheep Jones gone? I can't believe it."

Ganef was stirring again, muttering and shaking his head.

Cyrus was chanting the shrinking spell, but Beatrice asked him to stop. "Ganef just said something about Blacksheep, but I couldn't hear it. What happened to him, Ganef?"

"Goblins . . . beat me. I yelled . . . Blacksheep . . . wanted to warn him." The boy moaned and dropped his head. But then he forced himself to look at Beatrice again. "It was . . . a trap. They rushed me . . . goblins . . . twenty, maybe thirty—"

Ganef's head dropped again and he slumped forward. This time, it appeared that he had lost consciousness altogether.

"What did he mean about a trap?" Teddy asked anxiously. "Ganef? Tell us what happened!"

That's when they heard the faint sound of boot soles striking the stone floor. And then a voice that Beatrice knew well said from behind them, "I'll be happy to tell you everything."

Beatrice turned around slowly and looked into the eyes of her old enemy.

"Are you surprised?" Dally Rumpe asked. "I know you didn't suspect me. You *trusted* me, Beatrice Bailiwick, and that wasn't very smart. Not smart at all."

And then he laughed.

20

The Bailiwick Colors

Beatrice was staring into the handsome, smirking face of Blacksheep Jones.

She knew that the shock she felt must be obvious. He was right—she *hadn't* really suspected him—but now it all made sense. The highwayman was arrogant and egotistical, a loner, just as Dally Rumpe was. Even the alias he had adopted was telling. Bromwich had been the good brother and Dally Rumpe the bad one—the black sheep of the Bailiwick family.

Dally Rumpe had his sword drawn, the tip of it only inches from Beatrice's throat. He made a sudden playful jab at her and she couldn't help flinching. This delighted Dally Rumpe.

"So you thought you were going to win," he said gleefully. "You were just going to march in here and take everything away from me—and give it all to my brother." Now his dark eyes slid to Bromwich and his jaw tightened. "You didn't deserve to inherit Bailiwick," he said bitterly, his eyes blazing. "I was the older son. Bailiwick should have been mine. But you were *always* favored by our father. *'Bromwich is such a good boy,'* " Dally Rumpe mimicked nastily, " *'so kind, so talented. Dalbert, why can't you be more like Bromwich? Why are you so lazy? Why are you so bad?'"* Dally Rumpe's lips twisted into a sneer. "So where did being a good boy get you, eh? Two hundred years in the dungeon, while *I've* been living very well, indeed."

Bromwich was staring at his brother with a look of bewilderment on his face. Beatrice knew that he must be thinking, *How did this happen? How could he have become such a monster?*

Beatrice realized that she needed to keep Dally Rumpe talking, to give them time to think of a way out.

"Have you been living as Blacksheep Jones all these years?" she asked.

"Only the last twenty-five or so," Dally Rumpe answered, looking so pleased with himself it made Beatrice feel sick. "Being able to have anything you want becomes monotonous after awhile," he added smugly. "I needed some excitement in my life—and becoming the most daring highwayman to ever ride the roads kept things interesting."

"From what I hear," Pinchgutt said, eyeing the evil sorcerer with disgust, "Beatrice Bailiwick and her lot have made things *real* interesting for you."

Anger flashed across Dally Rumpe's face. "They're nothing but children! Pathetic, powerless witches who were stupid enough to believe they could beat me. But now," he added, his eyes glinting with triumph, "I'm going to make them disappear. Forever."

"Let them go, Dalbert," Bromwich said, looking steadily at his brother. "You can keep me, but let them return to their families. As you said, they're only children."

"*Annoying* children," Dally Rumpe replied coldly. Then his lips curved into a malicious smile and he began to strut around, his gaze shifting from face to face. "Let me see . . . How *shall* I do away with you? There are so many options. For example, I could turn you over to Zortag."

Dally Rumpe looked in the direction of the chained monster, who was now whining pathetically, and scowled. "No, Zortag has been a disappointment. He doesn't deserve the pleasure."

The evil sorcerer turned back to Beatrice. "I could set the goblins on you," he said brightly. "They would *love* that. They're very angry with you for leading them on such a merry chase. Or, perhaps, the Furies," he added slyly, looking now at a stone-faced Ollie.

Beatrice was standing next to Bromwich. While Dally Rumpe swaggered about, taunting them with the possible ways he could kill them, she reached for Bromwich's hand. She felt a slight squeeze of his fingers, as if Bromwich were saying he understood what she was about to do.

So softly that only Bromwich could hear, barely moving her lips, Beatrice began to chant:

By the power of whole,
By the beauty of the light,
Release this circle, I do implore,
Make all that's wrong revert to right.

By the power of the whole,
By the spirit of the wood,
Release this circle, I do implore,
Make all that's evil revert to good.

Then Beatrice had to stop because Dally Rumpe had walked back to her and was staring hard into her face.

"But perhaps the most appropriate punishment," he said, sneering again, "would be to imprison you all. That would give you lots of time to think about how foolish you've been." Then he shook his head vigorously. "No, no, no! I don't need any more prisoners. I don't need the one I've had for so long," he added, glancing at Bromwich. "Frankly, I've grown bored with it. I believe I'll march you all—including my dear, *good* brother—up to the moat."

He was grinning in near ecstasy, and Beatrice noticed that his face had begun to change. She knew what was coming. In a short time, the handsome mask of Blacksheep Jones would vanish, and Dally Rumpe would become his true self.

"Yes! That's what I'll do," Dally Rumpe chortled. "I'll watch while the goblins throw you to the hungry fish."

The sorcerer's jaw had begun to grow longer, while his tanned flesh faded to a gray pallor. As everyone watched in horrified fascination, the skin stretched tightly across the jutting bones of his face until it resembled a skull. Now sunken deeply into their bony sockets, Dally Rumpe's dark eyes glittered demonically at them.

"But enough of this chitchat," came the sorcerer's voice from that terrible face. He pointed his sword at Beatrice again and said, "Start walking."

With Dally Rumpe behind them, the tip of his sword pressed into Beatrice's back, they moved en masse through the archway and down the wide corridor. Beatrice was holding on to one of Bromwich's arms and Miranda the other, but the good sorcerer was so weak, he seemed barely able to pick up his feet.

If Dally Rumpe hadn't been breathing down her neck, Beatrice would have started whispering the rest of the counterspell to Bromwich, but she knew that wasn't possible now. Maybe before they reached the moat . . .

But Dally Rumpe seemed determined not to move an inch away from Beatrice. He kept prodding her with the sword, and whenever they reached a place where corridors turned or intersected, he would bark out directions. "Turn left!" "Go straight!"

They had passed the kitchen and were nearing the Treasure Room when Beatrice thought she heard muffled thumps. Once they were even with the Treasure Room door, she was certain of it. It sounded like someone was knocking against the old wooden door from the inside.

"Stop!" Dally Rumpe ordered.

No longer feeling the sword tip between her shoulder blades, Beatrice risked looking back. Dally Rumpe was turned toward the Treasure Room, listening, a glare on his hideous face. Then he stepped toward the door. At the same moment, Pinchgutt broke away and slipped through the wall into the Treasure Room.

Dally Rumpe roared and grabbed hold of the door handle. But before he could open the door, Pinchgutt had popped back though the wall, bringing Wolf Duvall and a string of thieves with him.

Dally Rumpe's eyes opened wide in surprise, and then narrowed as he barked, "Sword, engage! Pierce the heart of Wolf Duvall!"

Instantly, the sword flew from his hand, dangling in midair for a split second before zooming toward Wolf. The thief managed to block it with his own sword just before it sliced into his chest.

Beatrice and her companions were too startled by the arrival of the thieves to do more than stare as Wolf battled it out with Dally Rumpe's enchanted sword. The evil sorcerer was just as engrossed, grinning hideously as his sword backed Wolf into a corner.

Beatrice realized that Wolf didn't stand a chance of winning. The only hope they had against Dally Rumpe's magic rested in Beatrice's hands.

Over the sounds of clanking swords, she began to chant:

> By the power of the whole,
> By the chant of witch's song,
> Release this circle, I do implore,
> Make all that's weak revert to strong.

Watching the duel as she uttered the counterspell, Beatrice saw that Wolf had suddenly gained the advantage; now it was he who was advancing toward Dally Rumpe's sword. But then the enchanted sword made a powerful thrust at Wolf, and the thief's own weapon went flying from his hand.

"How dare you attack me?" Dally Rumpe hissed at Wolf, moving closer as his sword backed the thief against the wall. "I won't bother feeding *you* to the fish. I'll see you dead right now!"

The words began to tumble at top speed from Beatrice's mouth:

> *By the power of the whole,*
> *By the goodness of the dove,*
> *Release this circle, I do implore,*
> *Make all that's hateful revert to love.*

> *Heed this charm, attend to me,*
> *As my word, so mote it be!*

Its point now pressed against Wolf's robes, aimed directly at his heart, the enchanted sword began to quiver. Looking astonished, Dally Rumpe took a faltering step toward the thief. But in the next instant, the sword clattered to the stone floor, and Dally Rumpe fell in a heap beside it.

Shrieking with pain and rage, Dally Rumpe still struggled to meet Beatrice's eyes, his hatred burning into her face. Then his eyes suddenly rolled back into his head, and his body began to grow blurred. But, even then, Dally Rumpe wouldn't give up. His hand grabbed Beatrice's ankle, clutching it with amazing strength—until Ollie kicked it away. And as they all watched in silence, Dally Rumpe's body evaporated into a cloud of mist. The most evil sorcerer ever known in the Witches' Sphere was gone.

For a moment, no one spoke or moved. Then Pinchgutt turned to Wolf and said with a grin, "It's good to see you still know how to fight. I thought you might have forgotten, sitting in that fine house of yours while the rest of us do all the work."

"I'll be happy to take you on any time you say," Wolf said, returning Pinchgutt's grin.

Beatrice was confused. "But how did you know to duck into the Treasure Room?" she asked Pinchgutt. "Did you expect Wolf and the other men to be there?" Then she frowned. "You must have told Wolf what we were doing."

Pinchgutt looked sheepish. "All right, you caught me. But I got to worrying about a bunch of kids standing up to someone like Dally Rumpe—so I kind of mentioned to Wolf that we were going to the castle. And when I heard someone trying to break down the Treasure Room door, I figured it was him."

Beatrice didn't voice the thought running through her mind: *But you don't even like Wolf!* Obviously, that hadn't kept Pinchgutt from believing that Wolf would help them. And he had.

She turned to Wolf now and said, "Thank you. I don't know if we would have gotten out of this alive if you hadn't shown up. And we never would have made it to the dungeon without Pinchgutt and Badger!"

Badger's face flooded with color, but Beatrice could see that he and Pinchgutt were pleased by her words.

"I wasn't sure we could trust you," Beatrice admitted to Wolf. "It seemed like you had everyone in Heraldstone spying on us."

"That I did," Wolf replied cheerfully. "After meeting you, I had doubts about *you*."

"But they're all fighters," Pinchgutt said quickly. "Even the cat. She clawed that monster's face something fierce." Then he scowled at Beatrice. "It hasn't been all *that* bad working with you. You're pretty gutsy for a Reform witch."

Beatrice grinned and said, "It's been great working with you, too, Pinchgutt."

"Can you believe it?" Teddy said softly. "It's over. All five parts of the spell have been broken."

"And Dally Rumpe is gone for good," Miranda added.

Then Beatrice remembered Bromwich. Dally Rumpe had done terrible things to him, but the evil sorcerer was still Bromwich's brother. When she looked at Bromwich, she saw that he was smiling, but there was a shadow of sadness in his eyes.

"I'm grateful to all of you," Bromwich said, "more grateful than you will ever know."

Then he was hugging Beatrice and Miranda, and Beatrice could feel how desperately thin he was.

"So," Miranda said, glancing at Teddy after Bromwich had released her, "do you finally believe you can trust me?"

"I knew that a long time ago," Teddy replied, "when we were still back at Winged-Horse Mountain. I just figured if we ever did break the last part of the spell, you'd try to hog the spotlight. And I still have my suspicions about that."

"As well you should," Miranda replied. "I don't plan to play the shrinking violet when the reporters and photographers show up."

"What a surprise," Teddy muttered, but she was smiling. "You've turned out to be all right," she added.

"*Everything's* turned out all right. I just hope the Executive Committee finally breaks down and gives us our classifications."

Beatrice was still trying to fit all the pieces together. "Wolf, did you have any idea that Blacksheep Jones was really Dally Rumpe?" she asked.

"None," Wolf admitted, "and I've known Blacksheep for years. But he always operated alone, so we didn't really know what he was up to."

"I just remembered," Beatrice said, "Ganef is still locked up in the dungeon. We need to get him out."

"Absolutely," Bromwich said. "He shouldn't stay there a minute longer."

When they returned to the dungeon, Zortag had vanished. And Beatrice knew that every last goblin and Fury would have also disappeared with Dally Rumpe. The door to Ganef's cell stood open and the manacles hung empty against the wall. The young pickpocket was making his way slowly to the door, holding on to the wall for support.

"You did it," Ganef said weakly when Beatrice stepped into the cell. Then he looked shocked to see Wolf walking in behind her.

"Come on, my boy," Wolf said, "let's get you out of here."

He lifted Ganef into his arms and carried him out of the cell.

Beatrice looked down at Cayenne, who appeared tired and bedraggled. "I think you've earned a ride, too," Beatrice said.

Cayenne didn't have to be told twice. She leaped into Beatrice's arms and snuggled down with a weary sigh.

Ollie and Cyrus walked on either side of Bromwich, supporting him as they walked through the tangle of corridors and up the wide stone steps.

As Beatrice had expected, there wasn't a goblin or Fury in sight, but a great number of smiling, chattering witches had gathered on the main floor. When they saw Bromwich limping toward them, filthy and frail, but with his head held high, a silence fell over the crowd. Beatrice noticed that tears were running down many of the faces, and then a man near the back shouted, "Long live Bromwich!" and "Long live Beatrice!"

The rest of the castle staff began to chant the same words. Everyone was crying now, including Beatrice and her friends, and the men and women were bowing as Bromwich walked toward them.

"Stand up!" Bromwich called out to them. "Our days of bowing down are over."

Bromwich then walked among them, shaking hands and giving hugs, joy radiating from his haggard face.

"We must draw you a bath," one man said.

"And bring out your best robes," another added.

"And prepare a feast," a woman said as she dabbed at her eyes, "the finest Bailiwick has ever seen."

"Thank you," Bromwich said. "And could you take care of all my friends here? Show them to rooms where they can bathe and rest?"

Murmurs of "Certainly" and "Of course" ran through the crowd.

"And someone should go for Doc Llewellyn," Wolf said, looking down at the bruised and battered Ganef in his arms. "He'll need to see Bromwich and this boy—and maybe some of the others, too."

"I'll go," said a young man, and sprinted for the door.

The servants were all dashing around now, still wiping at their eyes, but long-suppressed laughter was heard, as well. Beatrice could feel their happiness swelling up within the castle walls, sweeping away all the terror and pain they had endured.

An older man had come to Bromwich's side and put an arm around the sorcerer's waist to support him.

"Honorius," Bromwich murmured, an especially pleased smile coming to his lips. Then his brows drew together in concern. "Was my brother cruel to you? Have the years been terrible?"

"Now that you are back, sir, those years are forgotten." The old man's face was radiant, even while his eyes brimmed with tears. "Let me help you to your chamber. And as soon as you've rested, I'll call in the barber."

Bromwich turned around to Beatrice and the others. "Come along, all of you. A bath and some clean clothing will do wonders for you."

Bromwich seemed about to say more, but then something outside the window caught his eye. Beatrice and her companions followed his gaze. It was morning, the autumn sun very bright after being in the dungeon.

Then Beatrice saw him. "Balto," she murmured.

Bromwich turned to her in surprise. "You know my horse?"

"We met him at Winged-Horse Mountain," Beatrice said. "Actually, he saved our lives."

She looked back out the window, smiling, then laughing out loud as she watched the beautiful winged horse fly over the wall and land in the castle yard. *You're as gorgeous and proud as ever, my friend*, Beatrice thought. And as if he had heard her, the white stallion threw his head back, white mane flowing like fine silk thread, and looked toward the window.

"Balto was staying with your daughter, Morven," Beatrice said to Bromwich. "So his being here probably means that all of your daughters are on their way."

For the first time, Beatrice saw tears come to Bromwich's eyes.

"How can I ever repay you?" he murmured.

"Come," Honorius said gently. "You need to rest."

"Just one moment more," Bromwich said softly, and pointed toward the tallest tower. "I've dreamed of this every day since my brother cast his spell."

Beatrice saw two men at the top of the tower. They had taken down Dally Rumpe's black-and-gold flag, and now they were raising the true Bailiwick colors.

Beatrice watched the flag inch its way skyward—the ruby-colored banner with the white winged horse in its center. Beatrice swallowed hard. She couldn't have spoken at that moment if she had had to. But there was no need for words. The Bailiwick colors flying again said it all.

21

Now What?

hen Beatrice, Teddy, and Miranda were
shown to their room by one of the
maids, they were too tired to fully
appreciate how grand it was. Cayenne leaped to one of
the ornately carved beds draped in rose and ivory silk,
gave a deep sigh, and immediately went to sleep.

What did impress the girls was the adjoining bathroom. It wasn't exactly modern, but there was a huge cop-
per tub, stacks of fluffy towels, and soaps that smelled
heavenly.

"A real bath," Miranda said with a groan of pleasure.
"I can't wait to wash my hair."

Then more servants arrived with trays of food, luxurious silk robes and slippers for the girls to wear, and even a
green velvet collar embroidered in gold for Cayenne.

"You should rest this afternoon," one of the women
told them, "because you're to be the guests of honor at a
banquet given by Bromwich this evening. And if memory
serves me correctly," she added with a glowing smile,
"Bromwich's banquets last well into the night."

After bathing, eating, and sleeping for a few hours, all
the girls, including Cayenne, felt almost as good as new.

Beatrice's shoulder was tender where Zortag had grabbed her with his claws, but she barely noticed as she slipped into the beautiful green robes Bromwich had provided. All Beatrice could think about were the butterflies in her stomach. She had a very bad case of nerves.

Members of the Witches' Executive Committee had always shown up after Beatrice and her companions had reversed a part of Dally Rumpe's spell, so she knew they would be at the banquet tonight. And now that they had broken the last part of the spell, the committee would surely announce Beatrice and her friends' classifications. If Beatrice were to be classified Classical, she'd have to make a decision. Would she enter a witch academy in the Sphere and prepare for a future in this magical world of Traditional witches (as well as ghosts and goblins, elves and giants, and every other sort of supernatural being one could think of)? Or would she decide to remain an ordinary girl in the mortal world—one who just happened to be a witch?

Beatrice glanced at herself in the oval looking glass in the bathroom, and was a little startled by what she saw. The girl staring back at her appeared confident and composed. And Beatrice thought that she looked older, too—not so much like a skinny eighth grader at John Greenleaf Whittier Middle School. More like—well, like a witch. Was it the lovely green robes that made the difference? Or perhaps, some magic in the looking glass? Or could it be that she *was* getting older, and beginning to grow into what she had been meant to be all along?

This thought caused Beatrice's heart to thump wildly beneath her robes. After a year of insisting that she didn't *want* to be classified Classical—that she would be perfectly happy being an Everyday witch and staying in the mortal world for the rest of her life—could it be, deep down, that she really did yearn for this new life that might now be open to her?

But wait a minute! She was getting as bad as Teddy—fantasizing about something that might never happen. There was no guarantee that the committee would give her a Classical classification, so it wasn't a good idea to get her hopes up. *If* that was what she was doing. *Was* she hoping? *Did* she want to be Classical? Beatrice stared hard at her reflection. The girl in the looking glass still appeared older—but also confused and worried, now, and more than a little scared. Because tonight her life might change forever. Or it might not. The trouble was, Beatrice didn't know *what* she was hoping for.

Teddy looked beautiful in her berry-red robes, and Miranda—who would look gorgeous in anything—was stunning in pale gray, the exact color of her eyes. Beatrice had brushed Cayenne until her fur gleamed, and the velvet collar sewn with gold thread added a regal touch that suited the cat.

When they met the boys in the hallway, Beatrice was blown away when she saw them. Cyrus's deep blue robes accentuated the color of his eyes and made him appear more mature. Looking quite handsome and distinguished in black, Ollie seemed destined for important things. And Beatrice noticed something else about her companions—instead of acting giddy with relief and excitement, as they usually did after they had bested Dally Rumpe, everyone was uncharacteristically solemn. *Could it be*, Beatrice won-.

dered, *that they're doing some serious thinking about their own futures?*

As they started down the wide marble staircase, Beatrice could feel the butterflies going berserk in her stomach. Ollie, who was brilliant and a leader in every way, certainly deserved a Classical classification. As did Teddy, who was probably as bright as Ollie and twice as driven. Miranda, too, was smart, not to mention being confident and sophisticated. And Cyrus . . . well, maybe he didn't have qualities that screamed *Excellence!* but in addition to being the most loyal friend in the world, he was always eager to take on any new challenge the Executive Committee threw at them, no matter how terrifying. All four deserved to be Classical. *But what about me?* Beatrice mused. She didn't have Ollie or Teddy's brilliance or Miranda's self-assurance or Cyrus's fervent desire for new experiences. And while the others had eagerly anticipated every trip they had made to the Sphere, Beatrice had dreaded them. The only reason she had come to the Sphere at all was because Bromwich and his daughters were in trouble, and they were family. That hardly seemed reason enough to justify making her Classical.

Then, as they reached the bottom of the stairs, something occurred to Beatrice that made her feel deeply ashamed. She really did want the best for her friends and her cousin, but what if *they* were classified Classical and she wasn't? How humiliating would *that* be?

Mobs of people were entering the castle and being directed to a room near the front doors, which stood wide open in welcome. Beatrice saw a lot of faces from Heraldstone in the crowd. There was Tom Duckham, the sheriff, walking with Lovie Fitzsimmons, and John Chew hobbling along with support from Doc Llewellyn. Beatrice recognized many of Wolf's thieves, as well, but she didn't know their names. She even saw Hobnob, still scowling, and looking around at everyone with great suspicion. All the guests were dressed in their very best for the occasion. Lovie was wearing crimson silk robes that were nearly as bright as her hair, and John Chew was resplendent in a new blue cape. Doc Llewellyn was still dressed in his usual drab tan, but he appeared somewhat cleaner.

Beatrice and her friends were soon swallowed up in the noisy, excited stream of new arrivals, and found themselves being swept into a huge room with a high domed ceiling. Tables as long as a football field were set with what looked like real silver plates and goblets, flickering candles, and banks of flowers in autumn colors. Hundreds of lit jack-o'-lanterns hovered over the table, singing— Beatrice did a double take, and satisfied herself that yes, the wide carved mouths were actually moving and a song about holiday fun was issuing forth from between their cutout teeth. That's when Beatrice remembered: Today was Halloween!

Men in finely tailored uniforms suddenly appeared beside Beatrice and her friends and escorted them to the head table, where Bromwich was already sitting with four young women. Beatrice recognized them at once, of course, as Bromwich's daughters. There was raven-haired Rhona from Winter Wood; Innes of Werewolf Close with brown hair; blond Ailsa from Sea-Dragon Bay; and Morven from Blood Mountain with red-gold hair. All the girls were talking and laughing, looking happier than Beatrice had ever seen them, and with good reason!

Then the four daughters saw Beatrice and her friends approaching, and rose quickly from the table to come meet them. The room was suddenly quiet, with everyone watching as Bromwich's daughters embraced Beatrice and her companions, their eyes bright with tears. No one could hear the hushed words exchanged, but long after the banquet was over, the guests would remember the pure joy that filled the room during this reunion.

Beatrice and her friends were led to Bromwich's table, and Beatrice was pleased to see that Wolf, Pinchgutt, Badger, and even a bruised but smiling Ganef were also at the head table, being treated as honored guests. Then Beatrice noticed that Lovie Fitzsimmons was sitting next to Wolf, her face lit up like one of the jack-o'-lanterns.

When everyone was finally seated, Bromwich stood and the room grew silent again. In his luxurious black velvet robes, Bromwich appeared gaunt and pale, but he was clean-shaven now so that everyone could see the radiance of his smile.

"My friends," Bromwich said, his voice surprisingly strong, "we are gathered here to *celebrate!* Dally Rumpe is gone, and Bailiwick is, once again, a united kingdom!"

Riotous cheers and applause rose from the assembled guests, and smiling as his eyes scanned the crowd, Bromwich waited patiently until they were quiet again.

"But most of all," the sorcerer was finally able to say, "we are here to honor the people who brought this all about—the brave and resourceful young witches who accomplished what almost everyone believed was impossible."

Then Bromwich began to speak the names, pausing slightly after each one. Beatrice Bailiwick. Teddy Berry. Ollie Tibbs. Cyrus Rascallion. Miranda Pengilly.

"I owe these young witches—everything," Bromwich said simply.

The cheers and applause this time were even louder.

Bromwich made a long speech, but no one grew tired of listening. They hung on to every word he uttered, nodding solemnly when he said that their rescuers had worked great magic, laughing with delight when he pointed out that Wolf and his men were the first thieves to actually be *invited* to the castle. Then Bromwich mentioned that Wolf's great-great-great-grandfather, Ebenezer Duvall, had been a respected adversary for many years—a man who had his own strong code of ethics and lived by that code—a man for whom Bromwich had felt great affection. When Bromwich added that Ebenezer would be proud of Wolf that day, Beatrice noticed that Wolf made a furtive swipe at his eyes.

Finally, Bromwich ended by saying that he hoped to convince Beatrice and her friends to remain at Bailiwick Castle, where they would be welcomed as beloved and honored members of his family.

After so much emotion, Beatrice felt drained, and she could see by the expressions on her friends' faces that they were feeling overwhelmed, as well. They were all grateful when trays heaped with food began to arrive at the table. And the food actually looked good!

Conversation turned lighter while they enjoyed the feast set out before them. Lovie had to lean over Ollie and Cayenne to inform Beatrice that Wolf had asked her to marry him.

"How wonderful!" Beatrice exclaimed.

"But you said you'd never have anything to do with a thief," Teddy reminded the tavern owner.

"And I meant it," Lovie declared, beaming at them. "But Wolf is giving up the outlaw life! We're going to open an inn in Heraldstone together."

Seeing the surprise on Beatrice's face, Wolf looked sheepish. "I told you that I had my own reason for wanting you to break Dally Rumpe's spell. Well, this is it. With Dally Rumpe gone, Heraldstone can become a prosperous town again. And with people coming from all over the Sphere on business, we'll need a fine inn."

Lovie was regarding Beatrice tenderly. "So I need to add my thanks to you. To all of you," she added, her misty eyes moving to take in all their faces. "As it turns out, Wolf has wanted to ask me to marry him for a long time, only he knew I'd say no as long as he was involved in thievery. But marrying an innkeeper is another kettle of fish altogether," she finished merrily.

"And Badger and I are going to be working at the inn," Ganef said, grinning. "Wolf and Lovie are paying us a lot more than we ever made picking pockets."

"But I've told them," Lovie said, her face suddenly fierce, "no sliding back to the old ways—and no explosions!"

"The explosions came in pretty handy last night," Beatrice said with a smile. "And what about Hobnob and Ludwig?"

"They'll work for us, too," Lovie said, appearing a little worried now. "But I don't think we'll let them have direct contact with the guests."

Good plan, Beatrice thought.

"What about you, Pinchgutt?" Ollie asked. "Are you going to work at the inn, too?"

Pinchgutt scowled. "Do I look like a chambermaid to you? No, I don't have any plans to change into a law-abiding citizen. *Ever!*" Then Beatrice thought she saw a twinkle in the thief's eyes. "Besides, now that Wolf's stepping down, I think I'm due for a promotion."

Wolf frowned and shot Pinchgutt a look. "Well, you'd better be doing your robbing outside of Heraldstone," he said, "because Bromwich has promised to bring in men to enforce the laws—and protect honest business owners like me."

Everyone had to laugh at Wolf's new-found virtue, even Pinchgutt.

About that time, Beatrice noticed Folly the ghost on the other side of the room, pouring a pot of soup over someone's head.

Lovie followed Beatrice's eyes and grimaced. "I guess we'll have to take Folly with us," she said grudgingly. "I mean, he really doesn't have anyplace else to go, does he?"

"He'll add some life to the inn," Teddy assured Lovie.

"More like chaos," Lovie replied with a sigh. "But witches *do* like to see a ghost or two when they travel."

"And Doc Llewellyn's going to retire," Ganef informed them. "He says he wouldn't miss the banquet for anything, but after tonight, if he never has to see the inside of this castle again, it'll be too soon. He's talking about building some condos—whatever they are—on Sea-Dragon Bay and learning to sail."

Somehow, Beatrice couldn't imagine Doc Llewellyn enjoying the feel of sea spray in his face. Or enjoying much of anything else, for that matter.

"What about John Chew?" Cyrus asked. "What's he going to do?"

Pinchgutt grunted. "Old John's like me, not about to change his ways. And I've told him he can hook up with *my* gang now, if he likes."

Wolf frowned and shot the thief another look. *Old habits die hard,* Beatrice thought with a grin. It was going to take awhile for Wolf to relinquish his dominant position in the outlaw pecking order.

Beatrice was refilling Cayenne's plate with creamed oysters and leeches when she realized that the banquet room had suddenly gone quiet again.

"They're here," Miranda said in a low, strained voice.

"I think I'm going to be sick," Teddy murmured, sounding scared to death.

Beatrice's eyes darted toward the door. And there they stood—thirteen witches who held her future in their hands.

22

Decisions

Bromwich rose from the table and went to meet the Executive Committee, moving slowly, but appearing quite stately in his flowing black robes. Everyone at Bromwich's table stood up and waited to see what would happen next.

What *did* happen was truly amazing, in Beatrice's estimation. Dr. Thaddeus Thigpin was leading the other committee members across the room. When he reached Bromwich, the Institute director looked for a moment into the sorcerer's glowing face, and then he embraced Bromwich.

Beatrice's mouth fell open, as did several others. Seeing the curmudgeonly Dr. Thigpin displaying emotions other than anger and scorn—and in public!—had to be a once-in-a-lifetime experience.

"Unbelievable," Teddy said flatly.

"I remember hearing that the Bailiwicks and the Thigpins had close ties," Wolf said, appearing surprised, nonetheless. "Bromwich was a good friend of Dr. Thigpin's great-great—uh, one of his ancestors."

"Well, then," Lovie said, dabbing at her eyes with a handkerchief, "this day must mean a lot to Dr. Thigpin personally."

Then Bromwich was leading the committee to the head table, and Beatrice's legs began to quiver. She noticed that Ollie's jaw was rigid, Cyrus's eyes were huge and round, and all the blood seemed to have drained from Teddy's face. Only Miranda—of course!—appeared calm and confident. But Beatrice knew better. With the possible exception of Teddy, Miranda was more anxious to hear the committee's decision about their classifications than anyone.

Beatrice's eyes sought out Dr. Featherstone and Dr. Meadowmouse to see if their expressions would reveal anything. They were gazing at Beatrice, as well, with big smiles on their faces. Then Peregrine poked his head out from between two of the taller witches and gave Beatrice the broadest and most crooked smile yet. Beatrice could tell that all three were proud of her and her friends—but she couldn't be sure of anything else. She was just going to have to wait.

Bromwich was requesting that a table for the committee be set up beside his own when Dr. Thigpin came to stand in front of Beatrice. He wasn't scowling at her, which was a unique experience for Beatrice, but he wasn't smiling, either. He just looked at her steadily, bushy white eyebrows drawn together, as if trying to solve an intricate puzzle. Then his hand shot out toward her.

Beatrice held out her own hand, feeling like she was in the middle of a dream as the Institute director shook it firmly, and said in a quiet voice, "Congratulations,

Beatrice Bailiwick. You and your friends have overcome incredible odds to reverse Dally Rumpe's spell and reunite the kingdom of Bailiwick, and you have all earned this committee's admiration."

"Hear, hear!" Dr. Meadowmouse exclaimed.

Dr. Featherstone was beaming, and some of the other committee members—who had pointedly ignored Beatrice and her friends up to now—were looking at the young witches with something close to interest in their faces.

"We're so proud of you, Beatrice," Dr. Featherstone burst out, as if unable to contain herself another second. "Your parents have been notified, and they're on their way here now. Dr. Thigpin sent an escort for them."

At this point, Beatrice *knew* that she had to be dreaming. First, Dr. Thigpin shakes her hand and actually congratulates her, and now he's invited her parents to come—*knowing* that her mother was banished from the Sphere twenty years ago—unfairly, in Beatrice's opinion, since her mother had done nothing wrong. But whether Beatrice agreed with the action or not, banishment was supposed to be forever.

"But—my mother—"

"I know, I know," Dr. Thigpin said impatiently, "she was banished because of that unfortunate incident when she was young. That's one of several things we've come to talk to you about." Now the corners of his mouth inched upward—painfully, it seemed—until he was almost smiling. "Our legal department has been working on your mother's case for some time, and we just received word that her banishment has been overturned. She can return to the Sphere any time she wants!"

Beatrice could hear her friends' excited murmurs and feel them patting her on the arm, but she was too stunned to respond. The banishment overturned? Could they do that? Being banished had caused Nina Bailey so much shame, she had never even spoken of it until Beatrice had found out on one of their earlier trips to the Sphere. This would mean everything to her mother!

"I can't believe it," Beatrice said softly.

"Oh, you can believe it," Dr. Thigpin said, sounding almost playful now. "If I tell you it's true, it's true."

A lump rose in Beatrice's throat and she swallowed hard. "Thank you, Dr. Thigpin," was all she could manage to say.

The Institute director appeared ready to speak again when Dr. Featherstone cried out suddenly, "There they are now!"

Beatrice's eyes followed Dr. Featherstone's gaze and she saw her mother and father standing in the entryway. It seemed that Dr. Thigpin had thought of everything because Beatrice's parents were wearing fine silk robes, her mother in forest green and her father in dark gold.

As Mr. and Mrs. Bailey were being escorted to the head table, Beatrice saw that her parents' faces were glowing. She started toward them, her vision blurred a little as her eyes filled with tears. Then her parents were hugging her, and all three were crying.

When Beatrice took their hands and led them to Bromwich's table, she realized that the room was totally silent. Glancing around, she saw that every eye was trained on the Baileys, and all the guests seemed to be smiling, even those who were wiping tears from their own faces.

Bromwich greeted Mr. and Mrs. Bailey warmly, Dr. Featherstone embraced them, and even Dr. Thigpin stepped forward to shake their hands. Beatrice couldn't be certain, but she thought she heard the Institute director say gruffly, "Of course you're proud. We're *all* proud."

Then Dr. Featherstone said to the Baileys, "You arrived just in time to hear Dr. Thigpin's announcement." And, turning to the Institute director, she added pointedly, "Weren't you about to tell Beatrice and her friends something else, Thaddeus?"

This prompting brought the scowl back to Dr. Thigpin's face, and Beatrice realized that she felt more comfortable seeing him in his natural state. But her friends were looking extremely tense, as were her parents. They were all staring holes through Dr. Thigpin, waiting for him to announce the classifications. Dr. Featherstone was obviously anxious for him to tell them *something*, and Beatrice knew her friends were taking this as a good sign. But Beatrice refused to grasp at that straw. She blew her bangs out of her eyes and looked out over the tables of guests, who also seemed to be waiting on pins and needles for the Institute director's next words.

"The committee has voted," Dr. Thigpin was saying, and Beatrice's eyes swung back to his face, "to add your cat's name to the official Animal-Familiar Register at the Institute."

Beatrice blinked. "That's—that's wonderful," she murmured, aware that Teddy and Miranda were looking at

Dr. Thigpin as if he had lost his mind—and possibly, as if they were considering an attack on his person. But Beatrice didn't take their self-involvement personally—and Cayenne certainly didn't. At this precise moment, Beatrice noticed, the cat was sauntering down the center of the table taking whatever appealed to her from other people's plates.

"She deserves it, Beatrice," Dr. Meadowmouse said earnestly. "And we've voted to add 'with honors' after her name. Very few animal-familiars have that distinction."

"She's a very brave cat," Dr. Featherstone agreed.

"Well, that's it," Dr. Thigpin said. "I've finished with what I had to say."

That's it? Teddy looked like she was ready to explode, and Beatrice certainly understood her friend's feelings. After all they had gone through—risking their lives over and over for a stupid test that Beatrice had never asked for, hadn't even *wanted*, and all he could say was *That's it?*

Beatrice cleared her throat and looked Dr. Thigpin straight in the eye. "There's just one more thing," she said, beyond caring whether she sounded impertinent or not. "You said after we broke Dally Rumpe's spell, we'd receive our classifications. Well—we've broken the last part of the spell."

"Indeed," Dr. Thigpin said, beginning to scowl again. "But Dr. Featherstone is in charge of witch classification. She'll let you know about all that."

Every eye in the room shifted to Dr. Featherstone, including Beatrice's. But Dr. Featherstone was no longer smiling. She looked positively somber. *What does that mean?* Beatrice wondered. But she knew. She thought now that she had *always* known. They hadn't beaten Dally Rumpe because they were great witches. They'd won through a combination of luck, perseverance, and the help of good friends. And the committee knew that. What choice did they have but to classify Beatrice and her friends Everyday?

"Let me read the committee's official statement on your classifications," Dr. Featherstone said, not quite meeting Beatrice's eyes. Then she looked down at the sheet of parchment in her hand. "*We, the below signed,*" she read, "*as active members of the Witches' Executive Committee, hereby officially record the outcome of our vote regarding the classifications of—*" Dr. Featherstone glanced up, and said, "All five of your names follow," and then looked back at the parchment.

But Beatrice was barely listening. She was thinking how odd it was to be feeling so much disappointment—so much *pain*—when she hadn't even known what she'd wanted to come out of this evening. But now she did know. Now that it was no longer a possibility, she knew very well. She *wanted* a Classical classification. She wanted to see if she could make it at a witch academy. The past year had been the most difficult of her life, but also the most exciting and challenging. She had learned so much about herself, and she wanted to learn more. She couldn't go back—she just couldn't! Not to pretending day after day that she was no different from the mortals around her. She *was* different. And that was okay. In fact, in the last couple of minutes, Beatrice had realized that her being different was *wonderful*. She wouldn't have it any other way. So what could she say to convince the committee? How could she change their minds?

"Beatrice!" Dr. Featherstone said sharply. "We seem to have lost you. But you need to listen to the part I'm about to read."

"Oh. Sorry." Beatrice turned her attention back to Dr. Featherstone. There would be time later to think about how to change their minds. Maybe there was an appeals process.

"*We, the members of the Witches' Executive Committee, vote to give all five candidates the same classification,*" Dr. Featherstone read, "*without restrictions or qualifications. The classification we believe to be most appropriate for the five candidates is—*"

Dr. Featherstone's head came up, and she finally looked into Beatrice's eyes when she said, "*Classical.*"

For a split second, no one moved. Then pandemonium broke out. There were shouts and screams and thunderous applause from the guests in the room. There were hugs and kisses from Beatrice's parents and from Bromwich and his daughters. There were grins and slaps on the back from Wolf and Pinchgutt, Ganef and Badger. And there was total shock in the faces of the five candidates.

Looking once again at Dr. Featherstone, Beatrice asked in a small voice, "Really?"

Dr. Featherstone nodded, smiling now, although she seemed to be fighting to keep her composure. But Beatrice decided that she must have been mistaken about that teary look in the older witch's eyes.

It was Teddy who began to cry—sob, actually—not seeming to care that her eyes were swelling and her nose was turning red. And Miranda just kept repeating, "Oh, my gosh, oh, my gosh, oh, my gosh—" while Ollie gripped Beatrice's arm so tightly he was cutting off the circulation, and Cyrus was swaying like he was going to pass out.

It took a full ten minutes for the guests to stop shouting and clapping, and for the five new Classical witches to regain control of themselves. Even then, Teddy was still breathing rapidly, and Beatrice and Ollie had to hold on to Cyrus to keep him from toppling to the floor.

"Perhaps," Dr. Featherstone said to Beatrice when the room was quiet, "you would like to know what affected our final decision."

"You know as well as we do," Dr. Thigpin said gruffly, "that you're no great shakes at magic."

Dr. Featherstone frowned at the director. "Magic is more than casting fancy spells," she said crisply. Then she looked back at Beatrice and her friends and blinked rapidly a few times. Yes, there really *were* tears in the older witch's eyes. "The first time we met you all—on your twelfth birthday, Beatrice—we told you that it takes more than spells to create magic. We said it takes courage—"

"And caring," Dr. Meadowmouse added.

"And perseverance," Peregrine squeaked.

"All five of you have shown that you have these qualities in abundance," Dr. Featherstone said, her voice quivering a little. "And you've succeeded where other witches, who were thought to be much more powerful, have failed. So every member of the committee agreed that we couldn't use a conventional yardstick for the five of you.

You've proven that you're great witches, whether your ability to cast spells is great or not."

"Not," Dr. Thigpin barked. "Definitely, *not*."

Ignoring the director, Dr. Meadowmouse held up a thick book with a black leather binding that was cracked and faded with age. It was *The Bailiwick Family History*.

"You know how this history always updates itself after you've broken part of Dally Rumpe's spell?" Dr. Meadowmouse asked, smiling at the five young witches. "You can read all the details of this trip later at your leisure, but I'd like to read the final paragraph to you."

Beatrice nodded shakily.

"As a result of your accomplishments to date," Dr. Meadowmouse said to Beatrice, "this is how you will be remembered years from now—no, *centuries* from now—in witch history. Of course, it's subject to change, based on how you live the rest of your life."

"I understand," Beatrice said.

"*Beatrice Bailiwick is known throughout the Witches' Sphere,*" Dr. Meadowmouse read, "*as a good and powerful witch—even though she has never been able to cast more than one kind of spell. But the stories of her victories over Dally Rumpe have been told and retold until everyone remembers only her courage, her loyalty, and her kindness, forgetting altogether her limited talent for traditional magic. Beatrice Bailiwick has her own kind of magic, and she has enchanted us all.*"

"Hmmm," Miranda said thoughtfully. "I wish that book could write *my* official biography."

"Remember, Miranda," Teddy said, cutting her eyes at Beatrice's cousin, "the book tells only the truth—*all* of it. Do you think your future public is ready for that?"

Miranda seemed about to glare at Teddy, but she ended up grinning instead. "Maybe you're right," she said blithely. "I'll hire my own ghostwriter and keep the really startling facts safely buried."

Food had been brought to the tables again. Beatrice's parents were seated on either side of Bromwich, and they and the members of the Executive Committee were more than happy to eat and relax a little. That gave Beatrice and her friends a chance to talk among themselves.

"Please don't tell me this is just a dream," Teddy said, "the result of too much chocolate before bedtime."

"If it *is* a dream," Beatrice said, "then we're all having the same one."

Teddy gave Beatrice a shrewd look. "You're happy about your classification, aren't you? You've finally decided that this is what you want."

"I am happy," Beatrice admitted, and realized suddenly that there wasn't a single butterfly left in her stomach. She smiled at Teddy. "And this is *exactly* what I want."

"When did you know for sure?" Cyrus asked.

"When Dr. Featherstone was beginning to read the committee's report," Beatrice answered, "and I thought they had voted the other way."

"I thought the same thing," Miranda said. "You could have knocked me over with a fairy wing when she said *Classical*."

"So," Beatrice said, looking around the table at her friends, "are we all coming to live in the Witches' Sphere?"

"Of course" and "You bet" everyone answered.

"What about you, Cayenne?" Beatrice asked.

The cat lifted her face from Teddy's plate and gave an emphatic meow.

"Well, I guess we're all in agreement," Ollie said with a grin.

"We'd better start looking at witch academies right away," Miranda said, all business again, "and decide where we want to go."

"Teddy might be able to help us there," Beatrice said. "She has a gazillion academy catalogs."

Miranda started asking Teddy questions about the academies, and then Cyrus jumped in with more questions, leaving Beatrice and Ollie to talk to each other.

"I was thinking," Ollie said, staring hard at the untouched food on his plate while the color rose in his face, "that I'd like it if you and I were at the same academy."

"Funny you should mention that," Beatrice replied, also staring at her plate, "because I was thinking the same thing."

They both looked up at the same moment and began to laugh when their eyes met.

"I *still* can't believe we're actually talking about going to a witch academy," Beatrice said. "I know my parents will be okay with it, especially now that my mom can come visit me anytime she wants."

Ollie reached into the pocket of his robes and produced a small package wrapped in cloth and tied with a piece of string. He held the package out to Beatrice, looking shy again, and said, "I was going to save this for a special occasion, but I can't think of a more special occasion than tonight. So happy Halloween, Beatrice! And happy Classification Day!"

Beatrice began fumbling with the string on the package while stealing glances at Ollie through her bangs. *What could it be?* she wondered. Her fingers felt clumsy because she was nervous, and it seemed to take forever to untie the string. But finally, Beatrice was able to fold back the cloth and see that Ollie had given her a silver bracelet with a charm attached.

"The castle," Beatrice whispered, her face lighting up with such obvious pleasure that Ollie stopped worrying about whether she would like the gift.

Beatrice held the bracelet up so that it caught the candlelight. "I saw this charm at the market," she said, her eyes resting on the tiny ruby in the flag, then moving to the white winged horse that looked just like Balto. She turned to Ollie and added, her face suddenly stern, "but it was *so* expensive."

"Not really," Ollie said, grinning. "I saw you looking at it, and I thought it would be a nice reminder of our time here."

Beatrice smiled and held out the bracelet so that he could fasten it around her wrist. She didn't tell him that she wouldn't need a reminder of this trip, that she would remember every moment of it for as long as she lived. Nor did she voice her other thought, that Ollie Tibbs made her feel happy and nervous and certain that everything would turn out as it should, all at the same time.

"There," Ollie said, closing the clasp on the bracelet.

"When we get home," Beatrice said casually, "why don't we borrow some of Teddy's catalogs and go through them together?"

Ollie was still holding her hand. He squeezed it now and said, "What good ideas you have, Beatrice Bailey."

Just then, Dr. Thigpin rose from the table and said that he wanted to make a toast.

"To the five young witches who sent Dally Rumpe packing," Dr. Thigpin said gruffly, "and to Beatrice Bailiwick—who has shown us all that she's anything *but* an ordinary, run-of-the-mill, Everyday witch!"

"Hear, hear," Dr. Meadowmouse said.

Beatrice Bailey's Magical Adventures

By Sandra Forrester

Beatrice Bailey stories are a combination of fantasy, whimsy, and high adventure guaranteed to keep young readers turning the pages. For Ages 10–14.

From the Reviews:

"Beatrice Bailey is a likeable character, charming without being overly so, and younger readers are sure to enjoy reading about her adventures… see how Beatrice Bailey grows and overcomes her obstacles."

— *Science Fiction Chronicle*,
August 2003

The Everyday Witch

ISBN 0-7641-2220-7
Beatrice Bailey is tall, skinny, and about to turn twelve years old. On that birthday she will get her official classification as a witch. Will she be named an ordinary "Everyday Witch" or a specially empowered "Classical Witch"?

BARRON'S
www.barronseduc.com

The Witches of Friar's Lantern

ISBN 0-7641-2436-6
Beatrice and her friends spend time in the village of Friar's Lantern, a town surrounded by eerie swamps and located uncomfortably close to a menacing neighboring village called Werewolf Close.

The Witches of Sea-Dragon Bay

ISBN 0-7641-2633-4
Beatrice and her friends Cyrus, Ollie, and Teddy are taken to a very unusual beach resort, where the waters are filled with sea serpents and monsters.

The Witches of Winged-Horse Mountain

ISBN 0-7641-2784-5
Beatrice learns that good and evil aren't always as clearly defined as she'd once imagined. If she chooses an evil path, she can defeat Dally Rumpe; otherwise, she seems destined to fail.

Each Book: Paperback $4.95, Canada $6.95

(#121A) R7/04